AVIATORS, ADVENTURERS, AND ASSASSINS

An Anthology of Novellas and Short Stories

S. Martin (Marty) Shelton

Captain USNR (ret.)

I dedicate this adventure book to those brave folks who tackle their quixotic adventures with confidence, foresight, and verve; to those who take decisive action to forestall manifest improbity; and to those who express their humanity with a touch of humor.

ACKNOWLEDGMENTS

Danielle Hartman Acee for her outstanding editing, project management, and promotion.

Doug Brown for his sterling cover and interior art.

Mike Cox for expert formatting of the photographs.

Marta Galvin for the eagle-eye copy editing.

Amanda Johnson *(nom de plume)* for her eagle eye editing.

TABLE OF CONTENTS

AMELIA

A *roman à clef*

Author's Notes

In this *roman à clef* novella I have assiduously presented the known facts of Amelia Earhart's mysterious disappearance in the Central Pacific during her 1937 around-the-world flight in her Lockheed Electra, Model 10E Special aircraft. She was en route from Lae, New Guinea, to Howland Island, near the Equator—the next to last stop before Oakland, the terminus of her flight.

The geography in my manuscript is reasonably accurate—as accurate as possible in a Mercator projection on a nine-inch by five-inch page. Most of the characters mentioned in this manuscript were persons involved in Earhart's around-the-world flight.

I've added an asterisk after key persons and equipment when first mentioned in the text to alert the reader to their images in the Photographic Gallery starting on page 57.

Prologue

I am Commander Richard Gregory, United States Navy—a Special Duty Officer, Intelligence. Currently, I work in the Office of the Director of Naval Intelligence (DNI) in Washington, D.C. Several weeks ago, the director ordered me to explore the Navy's involvement in the mystery surrounding the disappearance of Amelia Earhart* on her around-the-world flight during the summer of 1937.

The Chief of Information (CHINFO) has reviewed this manuscript and has authorized me to submit this unclassified version of my report to the Naval Institute for general release publication.

Tomorrow, 22 November 1944, I'm shoving off to the Central-Pacific. I have orders to report to Vice Admiral Marc Michener* aboard the aircraft carrier USS *Franklin** to serve as his staff intelligence officer.

Please note, following the conclusion of this manuscript, I've attached a Photographic Gallery that contains images of most of the people involved in this monograph and the equipment cited.

Background

Amelia Earhart, the celebrated aviatrix, gained fame in the 1920s and 1930s with her daring and record-setting aviation exploits. For example, in May 1932, she flew solo across the Atlantic—the first woman to accomplish this task. In July 1933, she broke the women's transcontinental speed record from Los Angeles to Newark. In January 1935, she was the first person to fly solo from Honolulu to Oakland.

The media published her dashing feats to full measure. We heard radio broadcasts announcing the new aviation records she set; we read the headlines in our daily newspapers, and viewed newsreel scenes of her latest achievement. She charmed the public with her boyish manner, genuine courage, and empathetic mien.

Amelia Earhart was born in Atchison, Kansas, on 24 July 1897. She had auburn hair and blue eyes, stood 5 feet 8 inches tall, and had a slim build. She married George Palmer Putnam* on 7 February 1931; he was a publisher, adventurer, and promoter. Putnam's genius for promotion and media manipulation had made her one of America's most famous and admired women.

Purdue University

On 24 July 1936, Doctor Edward C. Elliott*, President of Purdue University, invited Amelia Earhart to join their Engineering Department of Aeronautics as a technical advisor and visiting faculty member. Additionally, she was named a "counselor for women studies."

While associated with Purdue, Earhart developed the notion to fly around the world as close to the equator as possible. Putnam proposed that the university sponsor this flight. Convinced of the merit of Earhart's scheme, President Elliott created the Amelia Earhart Fund for Aeronautical Research. The fund's objective was to "finance the development of scientific and engineering data critical to the burgeoning aviation industry"—that is, to raise money for the aviatrix to purchase a Lockheed Electra Model 10E* aircraft, and pay for the expenses attendant to her around-the-world flight. University officials dubbed Earhart's Electra the "flying laboratory to garner aviation's unknown secrets."

The Lockheed Electra

Earhart's Lockheed Electra was an all-metal, twin-engine monoplane. To increase the Electra's range, speed, and load-carrying capacity for her around-the-world flight, Lockheed engineers made extensive modifications to the aircraft: installation of extra gasoline tanks, state-of-the-art electronic equipment, and more powerful engines. Amelia Earhart took delivery of her Model 10E Electra Special* on her 39th birthday, 24 July 1936.

Précis of Amelia Earhart's Around-the-world Flight

On 21 May 1937, Amelia Earhart and Fred Noonan*, her navigator, departed Oakland, California, in her Electra. She headed east to start her record-breaking flight. On 29 June she landed her Electra at Lae, New Guinea, an Australian Protectorate. She had flown for forty-four days and covered about 22,000 nautical miles. She and Noonan were physically and mentally exhausted.

Three days later, 2 July 1937, at 1000 hours, Earhart departed Lae, New Guinea, en route to Howland Island*, 2,230 nautical miles eastward. This area of the Central Pacific was mostly uncharted and was void of navigation aids. Her schedule was to arrive at Howland shortly after dawn the next day.

Howland Island, a United States possession, is a speck of an uninhabited island two miles long and one mile wide, and its highest point is ten feet above sea level. Howland was to be the next-to-last stop on her around-the-world flight. Noonan, using a sextant, celestial navigation tables, and his expert skills, was responsible for keeping the Electra on course (See Figure 1. Amelia Earhart's Planned Course on the following page).

The Coast Guard Cutter *Itasca**, Earhart's guard ship, was anchored on the northwest side of Howland Island. Her task was to provide Earhart with radio communication, radio directional beacon signals, and weather information. Shortly after sunrise, the *Itasca's* navigator spotted dark cumulus clouds building to the northwest. At 0742 hours local time, Earhart broadcast on 3105 KC, "KHAQQ calling Itasca. We must be on you but cannot see you. But gas is running low. Been unable to reach you by radio. We are flying at 1,000 feet."

Chief Radioman Leo Bellart*, aboard the *Itasca,* rated the signal strength of Earhart's transmission A5—loud and clear. That strong signal suggested that the Electra was within 200 nautical miles of the *Itasca.*

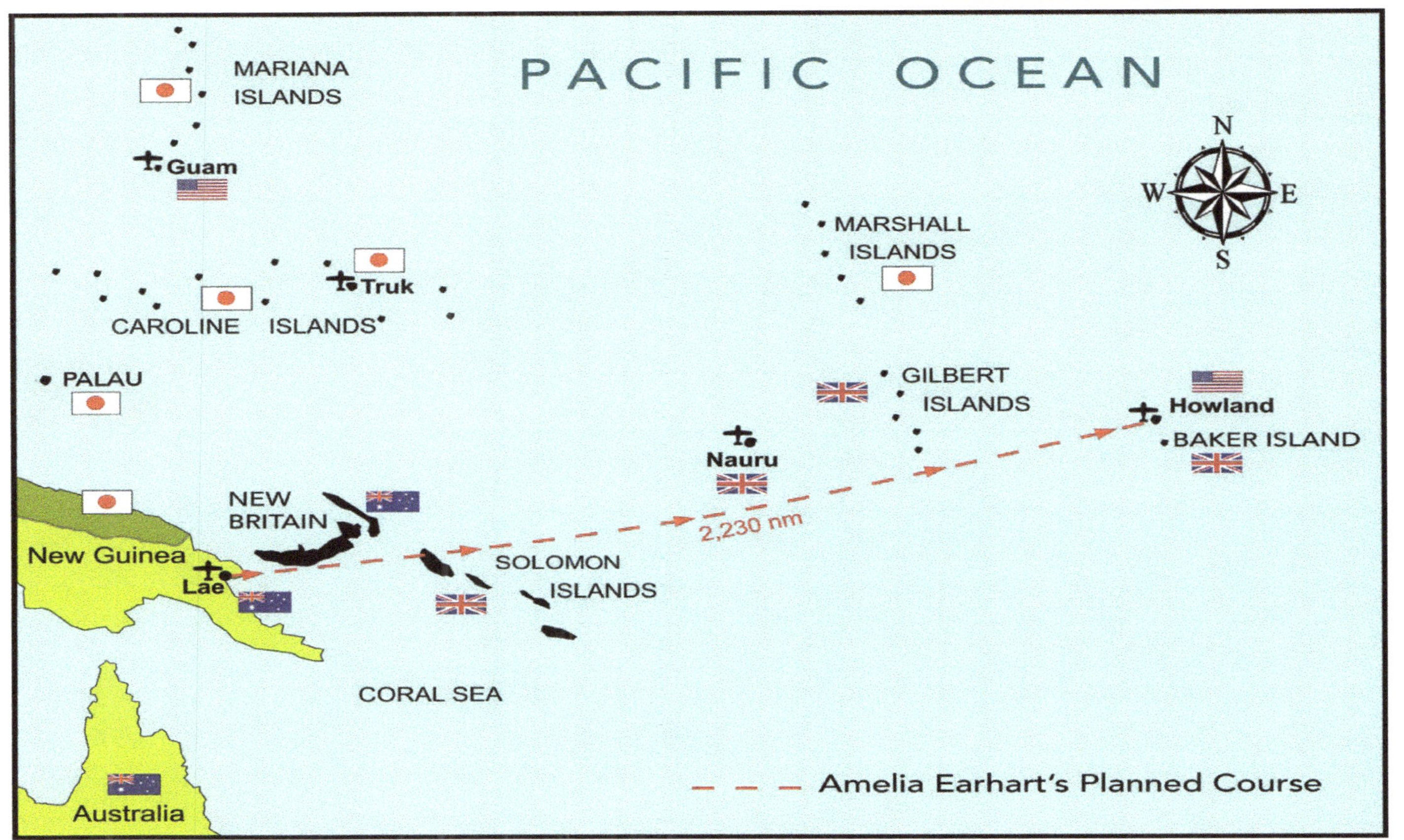

Figure 1. Amelia Earhart's Planned Course

Missing

As the morning developed, it became clear that the aviatrix had failed to find Howland Island. She and Noonan were lost and had disappeared. At 1040 hours, Commander Walter Thompson*, commanding officer of the Itasca, declared Amelia Earhart's Electra missing. He weighed anchor and began searching to the northwest of Howland Island—to no avail. The next day, President Roosevelt ordered a Navy task force from Pearl Harbor to join the search. Included were the battleship *USS Colorado** and its three scout aircraft*; the aircraft carrier *USS Lexington** and her eighty airplanes; three destroyers; and several support ships. The task force arrived on station in three days and began a comprehensive search.

In sixteen days, the Navy combed 140,000 square nautical miles. There was no trace of Earhart, Noonan, or the Electra: no life raft, no oil slick, no seat cushions, no scrap of clothing, no body parts. Nothing! Incredible! No flotsam from an aircraft crash into the sea. Can't be. There's always debris. Stuff remains on the surface for days even weeks—especially the oil slick.

Commander Pacific Fleet recalled its task force to Pearl Harbor. The Navy concluded, in its official report, that Earhart's Lockheed Electra had run out of fuel and crashed-landed in the Pacific Ocean somewhere northwest of Howland Island, and that Earhart and Noonan had perished.

Flight Analysis

To discover answers to the incongruities in the Earhart saga, I've analyzed technical facts attendant to her flight toward Howland Island. Some factors are inexplicable. For example, at 0730 hours local time, Earhart had been airborne for 19 hours and 25 minutes. The *Itasca's* radio logbook notes that in Earhart's 0742 hours broadcast she said that she was low on gasoline. An alternate *Itasca* radio logbook entry says, "Running out of gas only one-half hour left." It matters not which entry is correct. What's relevant is that the Electra's fuel tanks were almost dry. For several reasons, this message is troubling.

At departure from Lae, the Electra had 1,100 gallons of fuel on-board—enough for about 25 flight-time hours. Why then was the Electra fuel-starved on its arrival near Howland after only 19 hours flight? The Electra should have had enough fuel for about six or seven more flight-time hours.

This is the most vexing question about Earhart's last flight. What happened to those missing flight hours and that generous reserve of fuel? This discrepancy constitutes the essential mystery of Earhart's last flight.

We do not know the answer. But we do know that Earhart was determined to complete her flight as promoted and to arrive at Oakland on the Fourth of July. Her reputation demanded it. Her husband had arranged a gala reception for her, and she was under tremendous pressure to succeed.

Something Amiss

To this day, Commander Thompson's conclusions about Earhart's flight to Howland Island stand as the government's official statement. I'm not convinced. Official fog has obscured the underlying narrative of her flight. On its surface, Earhart's around-the-world flight had minimal aviation research practicality, and had no tactical or strategic interest to the Navy. Many senior officers and experienced aviators thought Earhart's flight was just a stunt to boost her career. Paul Mantz*, her mentor and former lover, dubbed her flight foolhardy. He averred that her minimal radio skills, refusal to learn Morse code, and arrogance probably precluded her from successfully completing this flight.

My curiosity was piqued by several discrepancies extant in the official conclusion. There is too much technical flimflam. Too much government involvement (dare I say "sponsorship"?) for an aviation stunt. For instance, why did President Franklin Roosevelt* authorize the expenditure of millions of scarce tax dollars, during the Great Depression, on this questionable civilian enterprise? He directed several civilian and government agencies to support her flight: arranging overflight clearances, clearing bureaucratic obstacles, building an airstrip on Howland, dispatching three Coast Guard cutters as Earhart's guard ships, and directing Pan American World Airways Pacific stations to provide weather information and to monitor her transmissions. Why was the U.S. Navy so keenly interested in Earhart's flight and engaged so massively in the search?

I propose that the answers to these questions lie in an official smokescreen that leaks volumes of the factual details of Earhart's last flight. I've integrated the known facts and discrepancies attendant to the Earhart tragedy into a likely scenario. I've concluded that the underlying motif lies in the Empire of Japan's chicanery in the central Pacific.

Japan and Micronesia

To set a perspective for the martial undercurrent that infused Earhart's last flight, I'll review the historical context of the times.

A few days after the start of World War I in August 1914, Great Britain urged the Empire of Japan to declare war on Imperial Germany. Japanese marines in concert with British colonial forces captured Tsingtao, the primary German treaty port in China. The German East Asiatic Naval Squadron, which consisted of two armored cruisers, the *SMS Scharnhorst** and the *SMS Gneisenau,* and four light cruisers, escaped the Japanese naval blockade and steamed toward Germany's colonies in Micronesia. An Imperial Japanese Navy task force, led by the battle cruiser *IJN Shikshima**, pursued the escaping German squadron with the ostensible goal of destroying it, thus ensuring safe passage for Allied commerce in the central Pacific.

However, when the Imperial Japanese Navy reached Germany's Pacific Ocean possessions in the central and southern Pacific, they abandoned the pursuit and let the German squadron sail eastward towards Frederikshavn, their home port.

The Great War ended in November 1918. As part of the Treaty of Versailles, the League of Nations* mandated the German Pacific colonies (Micronesia) to the Empire of Japan with the provisos that:

Japan would keep this area of the central Pacific open to foreign commerce and navigation.

Japan would not annex or militarize these islands.

Administer these territories as a sacred trust to develop them for the benefit of the native peoples.

These mandated islands in Micronesia are a sprawling chain of volcanic islands and coral atolls lying about 2,300 nautical miles astride the central and southern Pacific. They range from Saipan in the Marianas to Mili Atoll in the Marshall Islands, Truk in the Carolines, the Palau Islands, and the New Britain archipelago.

See Figure 2 on the following page, League of Nations Mandated Islands.

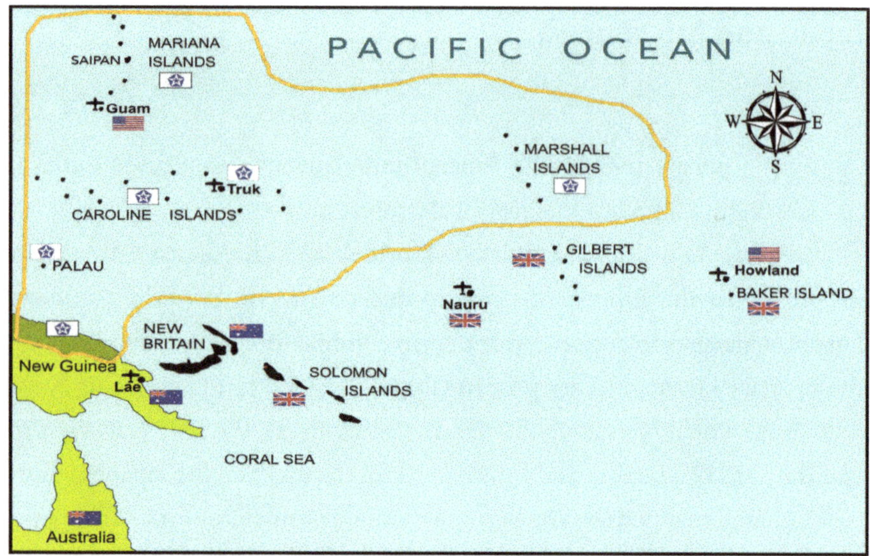

Figure 2. League of Nations Mandated Islands

In February 1933, the Empire of Japan* decamped from the League of Nations, and refused to surrender Micronesia. No Western nation had the will or capability to challenge this Oriental empire. In blatant disregard of the League's provisos, the Japanese sealed Micronesia from foreign shipping and visitors, and established a "Bamboo Curtain" surrounding the area. Unauthorized intrusions were met with military force.

Behind this Bamboo Curtain, the Japanese Navy began an aggressive program to build naval bases, airfields, and defensive fortifications throughout Micronesia: on Jaluit and Kwajalein in the Marshalls; on Truk and Yap in the Carolines; and on Tinian and Saipan in the Marianas.

On reflection, we now realize that the occupation and fortification of Micronesia was the Empire of Japan's first-stage preparation for their upcoming war with the United States and the colonial powers in Asia for control of the Pacific Rim. Japan's long-term goal was to implement its classified Greater East Asia Co-prosperity Sphere policy by ridding Asia of Occidental political, economic, cultural, and religious influences, and to create a group of self-sufficient Asian nations under Japanese autocracy.

In effect, the Empire of Japan proposed to control and harvest the rich natural resources of the Pacific Rim that the home islands lacked: petroleum from the Dutch East Indies, rubber from Indochina, tin and palm oil from Malaya, copper and gold from Portuguese Timor, iron ore and rare-earth elements from China, hardwood timber from Burma, and magnesium and zinc from Siam.

See Figure 3, The Empire of Japan's Greater East Asia Co-prosperity Sphere.

Figure 3. The Empire of Japan's Greater East Asia Co-prosperity Sphere

Their strategic plan also included occupation of British Singapore to control the vital shipping lane the Strait of Malacca.

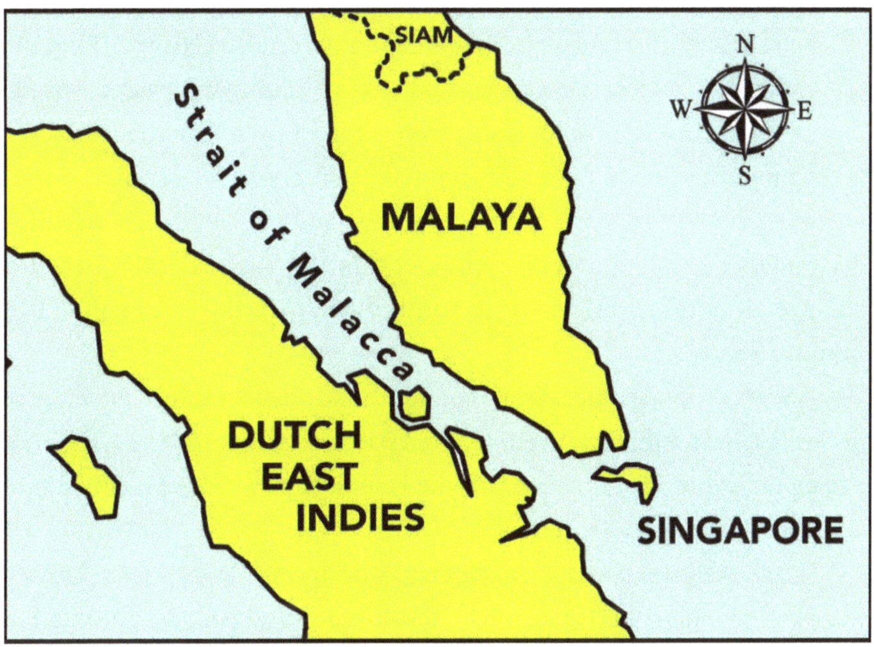

Figure 4. Strait of Malacca and Singapore

Naval Intelligence

The U.S. Navy had no dedicated human intelligence (HUMINT) assets and only a minimum skills capability of obtaining information inside the Bamboo Curtain. Nonetheless, from time to time, our naval attachés throughout the Far East got human intelligence reports from missionaries returning home, defecting Korean workers, and the few Malaysian rubber traders permitted into the area. Occasionally, such HUMINT yielded a nugget of information. However, for the most part, this information had minimal value.

Several clandestine operations were conducted to gather intelligence on the Japanese militarization of Micronesia. For example, sub rosa, a special naval postal unit read the mail that the Honolulu post office processed into and out of the Bamboo Curtain.

One valuable source of human intelligence came from Marine Lieutenant Colonel Earl (Pete) Ellis, USMC*. He had earned a chest full of medals in the Great War. After the Armistice, the Navy sent him on a number of attaché and reconnaissance missions into the Orient. He spoke Japanese fluently. On his return to our offices in Washington, he drafted the definitive study on Japanese activities and intentions in the Pacific, and he detailed with prescient accuracy our ongoing war with Japan for control of the Pacific.

In the early 1920s, Colonel Ellis penetrated the Bamboo Curtain as a representative of the Hughes Export Corporation of San Francisco a Howard Hughes* shell company used as a cover for American intelligence operations. Ostensibly, this outfit dealt in rare-earth elements and other exotic minerals. After a dozen or so cables in a non-obvious book code, Ellis went silent in May 1922. We suspected that the Japanese counterintelligence, the Kenepitai*, captured and beheaded him—somewhere on Palau in the Carolines.

In 1932 our submarine *USS S-48* took periscope photography of the burgeoning Japanese naval base at Truk, but the results were of minimal value.

In the 1930s, Lieutenant Joseph (Joe) Rochford, USN*, operated a Top Secret signals intelligence operation (SIGINT) dubbed Station HYPO, at Pearl Harbor. Navy cryptographers monitored Japanese navy radio transmissions and worked to break their codes and read messages. Rochford's operation had some measure of success.

Assessing the Empire of Japan's aggressive behavior and the contentious diplomatic tensions in the Pacific, the admiralty knew to a near certainty that a Pacific war was inevitable. What scraps of intelligence the Navy had about Japan's secret preparations inside the Bamboo Curtain were mostly unverified and outdated. By 1933, the status quo was untenable. The Commander in Chief of the U.S. Fleet, Admiral William Standly, USN*, issued an Operations Directive, classified Top Secret, to the Director of Naval Intelligence, Captain Hayne Ellis, USN*, ordering him to increase surveillance of Japanese military activities in Micronesia and submit timely Essential Elements of Information (EEI) reports.

Unfortunately, our Naval Intelligence did not have the expertise or technical know-how to implement Admiral Staley's directive to any degree of satisfaction.

As the years passed, Japan became increasingly more aggressive. By July 1937, the Japanese Kwangtung Army* had seized Manchuria and were waging an intensive campaign in China. They had captured Peiping, Nanking, Tsingtao, Shanghai, Canton, and the Kwangtung Peninsula.

That was how the Pacific was roiling when Earhart made her last flight.

Director of Naval Intelligence

In February 1941, with war in the Pacific looming, President Roosevelt, the National Command Authority, and Admiral Ernest J. King, USN*, the Commander-in-Chief, of the U.S. Fleet, put intense pressure on Admiral Alan G. Kirk, USN*, Director of Naval Intelligence, to get hard intelligence about Japanese activities in Micronesia. What intelligence the Navy had was unverifiable and old—not the sort of information to present to the President.

One morning in early March 1941, Admiral Kirk summoned me to his office. Here's an approximation of our conversation. Without ado he snapped, "Commander Gregory, my butt is in a sling and the poohbahs upstairs are beating it. We need A-1 intelligence on what the Japanese are doing in Micronesia and I'm at a loss on how to get it." He took a long draw on his ever-present cigar. His eyes followed the exhaled smoke as it drifted slowly upward.

I knew his moods. He was thinking and did not want to be interrupted.

He looked at me with a quizzical eye and swigged his coffee. "I read your treatise on Amelia Earhart's trans-Pacific flight in 1937. I was intrigued by your analysis of her fuel consumption conundrum. Well done." He paused for a few seconds, put his elbows on his desk, and leaned towards me. "I read in the subtext of your paper that Amelia Earhart might have diverted her Electra into Japanese Micronesia. Do you have something I can use? Exploit? Anything hard?"

"Perhaps, Admiral." I shifted forward in my chair and looked him straight in the eyes. "There's something seriously amiss about her flight. I have no firm answers, but I have an inkling of what happened."

"An inkling? Not good enough, Commander. I need hard, verifiable intelligence that I can hand to Admiral King so he can brief the President. And I need it ASAP or sooner. Reckon you can transmute that inkling into A-1 intelligence?"

When an Admiral puts on the pressure, you'd best have the answer. "Aye, aye, sir," I snapped. "I'll need…"

In a booming voice he interrupted, "I don't give a damn what you need! Get it. I'll have our administrative officer cut orders that'll allow you to proceed to wherever you need to go 'as you've been verbally instructed' and with top priority air transport. All expenses authorized." He went to his safe, twirled the dial, swung the door open, scanned a few lines in a binder, and closed the safe. Without ado, he snapped, "Your project is classified Top Secret, special compartment intelligence MERCURY. Shove off, Commander. Keep me posted."

The Search

For several weeks I searched documents at the Library of Congress and National Archives for evidence of our government's or the Navy's involvement in Amelia Earhart's last flight. I scanned probably a thousand index cards by major and minor subject listings. I searched every conceivable lead. I found mostly public information and a few lightly classified documents of no import. This search tack was a void.

As I was about to give up searching the National Archives and move to another search venue, I decided to take one last look in one of its highly-classified vaults. After four more hours of frustration, I had not seen anything relevant, and I was ready to return to the office. As I rose to an upright position, I spotted a small, red-striped box lying catawampus at the rear of an adjacent shelf. I got it.

This box was sealed with heavy-duty tape and marked "DO NOT OPEN WITHOUT AUTHORIZATION." *What the dickens. Who's supposed to authorize the opening?* I looked about. There was no one in the vault, so I authorized myself to open the box. I slit the tape with my pocket knife. Inside was a pile of mostly unclassified and irrelevant documents from the Naval Air Station Alameda, California, that had no reason to be in this vault. *Why is this box so highly classified?* Eventually, I found the answer. In my hand was a sealed envelope stamped "TOP SECRET MERCURY." *Mercury? Bingo! Could be.* I cut the seal and removed a paid receipt from the Fairchild Camera Corporation for a KA-17 aerial camera*, serial number FC327; a 24-inch Zeiss Planar lens, serial number 2385; a 200-foot film magazine, serial number 184; one Eastman Kodak starburst K-2 filter; and a 200-foot packet of nine-inch Kodak Plus X aerial film ASA 100. Handwritten on this receipt was, "Paid $1,337.00 in cash." The receipt was signed, "Sydney J. Kellogg, Jr., Vice President, Fairchild Aerial Camera Division." Below that was the notation, "Received in good order, Commander Russell R. MacCleaver, USN, Supply Officer, USNAS Alameda." The date on this receipt was 11 May 1937.

"Bingo!" The date was right on target, and the aerial photographic equipment had been paid for in cash. The military never pays cash for anything unless the transaction is sub rosa.

The next day I was in Admiral Kirk's office. Hearing my report, he cracked a small smile. "You're on to something. Follow through and find out if this aerial camera has anything to do with Earhart's flight."

"Aye, aye, sir."

From this evidence, it appeared that some government muck-a-muck had tasked the Navy with managing some sort of clandestine aerial-reconnaissance operations. The peacetime Navy would never undertake such a risky venture without a presidential directive. At the time, military budgets were tight, Congress was saturated with isolationists, and the public were more interested in surviving the Great Depression than in Japanese Micronesia.

The Hunt

I checked with the Office of Naval Personnel to find the whereabouts of Commander MacCleaver. The yeoman, in her return telephone call, told me that Russell MacCleaver was killed in the crash of a PBY Catalina* patrol plane near Midway Island last year.

To follow the next lead, I commandeered a Beechcraft SNB*, twin-engine utility aircraft from Naval Air Station Anacostia and flew to Hartford, Connecticut. I landed on the runway at the Fairchild Aviation Corporation plant. The personnel director did not want to discuss their employees. I told her I was on a mission of national importance and it was critically important for to me interview their employee Sydney J. Kellogg. The woman was unimpressed and still refused my request. With as much élan as I could muster, I told her, "I'll return this afternoon with a federal search warrant and a cadre of federal marshals to find him." Her eyes narrowed, and she wiped her brow and snapped, "Federal blackmail is tawdry."

Without ado, she left. About fifteen minutes later she returned with a slip of paper. Standing just a couple of feet in front of me she said, "Commander, here's what we know about Sydney J. Kellogg. He retired sixteen months ago. We have no information about his location." In stoic silence, she returned to her desk, lit a cigarette, leaned back in her chair, and began, in a more conciliatory voice, "I've heard a rumor that Kellogg is working for the Hughes Tool Corporation somewhere out West." She paused, scanned the slip, and continued, "No one at this plant knows about the sale of that KA-17 camera to the Navy. It must have been one of those off-the-record deals that he alone negotiated."

Next day, I was en route to Los Angeles on an Eastern Airline DC3*, bound for the personnel department of the Hughes Tool Corporation. The personnel manager said unequivocally, "There is no Sydney J. Kellogg working for us. And we've never had such a person on our payroll." He rose, extended his right hand, and said, "Good day, Commander."

As I drove back to my hotel, my synapses crackled with suspicion. *Something is askew. I've found excellent starting clues to my research. Yet my follow-on inquiries have hit deathly silence. This scenario is too scripted.* I reviewed the reasons why the Navy would covertly purchase that Fairchild aerial camera in mid-1937. One possibility stood above all others: to install it in Earhart's Electra.

Next stop was the Naval Air Station (NAS) Alameda—across the Bay from San Francisco. If the Navy had installed the Fairchild aerial camera in Earhart's Electra, it was probably done at Alameda. It's only a few miles from the Oakland Airport, which was Earhart's home base and starting point for her around-the-world flight.

I called my office, and told Intelligence Yeoman Don Pickart to have the Special Security Group at Naval Intelligence headquarters forward my security credentials via the "back channel" to their counterparts at NAS Alameda.

Prior to World War II, Naval Air Station Alameda, was the home base for several seaplane and utility squadrons. My research confirmed that there were no aircraft capable of precision, stereo-aerial photography stationed permanently at this base. In a curious twist, this station was also Pan American World Airways'* terminal for its China Clipper trans-Pacific operations.

Pan American World Airways

The intrigue deepened. Pan American's China Clipper* service started in 1935, during the heart of our Great Depression. Pan American gained landing and terminal rights at the Naval Air Stations at Alameda, Pearl Harbor, Midway, Wake, Guam, and Subic Bay in the Territory of the Philippines. From Subic Bay, the Clipper ships flew to Portuguese Macao or to British Hong Kong, either city being the terminus of their trans-Pacific route.

The pertinent questions were, how did Pan American finagle these landing rights and finance this costly operation—purchasing expensive flying boats and establishing an extensive network of bases consisting of employees, supplies, structures, and equipment—and expect to turn a profit on the income of a few high-fare passengers and mail contracts? The plausible answer is that it did not.

Accordingly, the reasonable explanation was that our government financed Pan American's trans-Pacific operations: the China Clipper route. President Roosevelt must have reasoned that it would be in the country's national interest to have a direct route to the Orient, one that skirted the Bamboo Curtain. In a hidden budget, he could have channeled the funding for the purchase of twelve Boeing Airplane Company model 314 Flying Boats* and the attendant operational cost. He must have guided this secret funding into Pan American via Juan Trippe, president of the airline and his close friend. In a classified Executive Order, the President would have ordered the Navy to make their air stations and seaplane bases available to Pan American, with Alameda the hub of the China Clipper operations.

NAS Alameda, *Continued*

Shortly after morning colors, I was in the office of the commanding officer of the Naval Air Station Alameda*. Also present were his security officer and the aviation maintenance officer. After the introductions, coffee, and obligatory small talk, the skipper said, "We'll help any way we can, Commander. But all of our older aircraft maintenance records were either destroyed in a fire several years ago or sent to the National Archives last year. Since we received your arrival message, I've had our people search every office and hangar on this station. We didn't find any records about modifying a civilian airplane on this station."

Not to be deterred, I asked, "I appreciate your thorough investigation. I was counting on finding some documents relevant to my investigation. With your permission, may I stay a few days and wander about your station?"

"Yes, Commander. Lieutenant Edward Ruhnke, our maintenance officer, will be your escort."

"I ask that you keep confidential my visit here."

"Of course."

I addressed Lieutenant Ruhnke, "Where shall we start?"

His eyes narrowed as he reviewed the options. After a few seconds he said, "We didn't search that derelict hangar on the east side of the field. It's a real dump and too dangerous to enter. It's private property, and we do not have permission to enter or instructions on what to do with it. It's Off Limits to all hands."

That's a puzzlement. What's abandoned private property doing on a naval air station?

"Skipper, with your permission, I want to look inside this hangar."

A slow smile crept across his face as he glanced at his watch. "I've a meeting to attend. Enjoyed meeting you, Commander." He and the security officer left the room.

I've seen several "no attribution" scenarios in my career; this was a classic. I addressed Lieutenant Ruhnke. "Let's go."

En route in a station pickup truck, Ruhnke said, "Perhaps I should have mentioned that I suspect that the Hughes Tool Corporation* owns this hangar. I've spotted a few scant clues in what base maintenance records are left."

I interrupted him with a resounding "What!" *The plot thickens.* "Tell me more."

He looked at me with wondering eyes and continued, "All we know for sure is that Hughes Tool built this hangar in the mid-1920s—to what end, we do not know. Hughes abandoned it shortly after the war started and their crew left the station without instructions on its disposition. We've contacted the Navy's Engineering and Facilities Command in D.C., and they claim to know nothing about this hangar. We've queried people in the Hughes organization to no avail—the silence is deafening. Because it's such a safety hazard and eyesore, we've taken the initiative and hired a contractor to demolish it. We expect that crew here next Monday."

Ruhnke was right. The Hughes hangar* was a dump. The large double doors were askew, part of the roof had caved in, and most of the windows were broken or knocked out. Debris of all manner littered the concrete floor. It was precarious just to navigate through the scrap.

After several hours of searching every office, nook, and cranny, I had found nothing related to Earhart or her Electra. After a thermos of coffee, it was time to recycle the liquid. I kicked open what was left of the door on the men's head ("men's room" for civilians). Yes, I knew it was not in working condition, but nature's call must be satisfied. As I was leaving, I spotted a maintenance closet. It was difficult to see because it was off to one side and in almost complete darkness. Surprisingly, the closet's door was secured with a heavy-duty padlock.

With the assistance of a metal beam salvaged from the debris, Ruhnke and I destroyed the door. Scattered about inside were boxes of cleaning supplies and related paraphernalia. Toward the rear was a dust-covered, four-drawer, rusted metal file cabinet. With minimal effort, we got the top drawer opened. Inside was a random jumble of miscellaneous paperwork: personnel documents, transfer orders, Judge Advocate issues, medical records, notations of visiting aircraft, and aircraft maintenance logs. These documents spanned the period from the late 1920s to 1939. No more tingling. Another bust. We were about to leave when some compelling prescience that I cannot explain urged me to examine that aircraft maintenance drawer again, this time much more carefully. After a frustrating hour—nothing. I slammed the drawer shut. With an expletive not appropriate for the readers.

As I backed away from the filing cabinet, I saw the bottom drawer slowly slide open. Reckon the energy of my slam had a dual effect. Toward the rear was a file I had passed over too hastily in my first search. In an almost illegible cursive, the file was captioned in a faint pencil scribble, "Electra," and it was dated "17 MAY 1937." "Bingo!" I shouted.

Inside was documentation recording the installation in Earhart's Electra Model 10E Special, Civil Aeronautics Authority registration number NR16020, of an aerial camera suite. Included were one Fairchild KA-17 aerial camera BUAER serial number FC327; a nine-inch film magazine, BUAER number FM184; and a Zeiss Planar 24-inch lens, BUAIR serial number 2385, with a Kodak K2 starburst filter installed. These serial numbers matched exactly those on the invoice I had found in the National Archives.

Also in the file were oaths signed by all personnel involved in this camera installation, swearing them into the intelligence-compartmented program "TOP SECRET MERCURY." One sentence stood out in bold, larger type: **"YOU ARE BOUND BY THIS OATH UNTIL A SENIOR NAVY INTELLIGENCE OFFICER RELEASES YOU FROM THIS OBLIGATION."** I pulled all the paperwork from this file and carefully stowed it in my briefcase.

Given this tantalizing documentation, I figured there must be more information in the mysterious file cabinet. I opened the top drawer, where the personnel records were up front, and I carefully scanned every file in the drawer. Nothing of use. Next, I opened the third drawer and looked at each folder. I passed one folder tabbed "Naval Reserve Personnel." Nothing again. I closed the drawer. With a what-the-hell attitude, I refused to acknowledge that there was nothing more for me here. I opened that third drawer again and scanned every page in every folder, finding Hughes Tool pay records, flight-time certificates, physical examination records, and enlistment and discharge papers. And then, there it was! Amelia Earhart's signature on a certificate commissioning her as a Lieutenant in the Naval Reserve, and the record of her physical examination. She had not been authorized to wear a uniform and was not issued an ID card.

Also in this file was the record of Fred Noonan's participation in the Naval Reserve program as a Lieutenant Commander. His designator was 1635, a Special Duty Officer, Intelligence Specialist. *Noonan an intelligence officer!* My neck tingled with intensity. On reflection, I should not have been surprised. As a merchant-marine master, Noonan had to be a Naval Reserve officer. But the SDO Intelligence designator added an intriguing twist to the enigma of Earhart's disappearance.

The clues were building, and confirming that I was on the right track. Our government, and the Navy in particular, had been prime participants in Earhart's last flight. It was obvious that the Navy had sent her on an aerial reconnaissance mission. That's why her last flight was couched in such a highly-compartmented intelligence classification. But the question now was, what was her target? I had a notion, but not enough evidence to confirm it or to present it to the Admiral.

I was thrilled at this treasure trove find but seriously troubled at seeing these highly classified documents in an unsecured location. There was no apparent reason for it. Perhaps it was an oversight in the hubbub of abandoning this hangar. The Howard Hughes outfit was notoriously careless with paperwork.

The White House

By early April, I was back in Washington at Naval Intelligence Headquarters. I briefed Admiral Kirk and showed him my documentation. He smiled again and said, "As I suspected. She took reconnaissance photographs of something. Find out what."

"Aye, aye, sir."

The next step was obvious. An Amelia Earhart reconnaissance mission into Japanese Micronesia would have to have presidential authority. With minimum effort, I found that Amelia Earhart had visited the White House on 21 December 1936. I called the Secretary to the President, James Roosevelt* (his oldest son), to arrange an appointment to discuss Earhart's visit.

"Okay, Commander. Come by about 10:00 o'clock tomorrow morning. I'll set up your clearance and see what I can find."

On time, I entered Roosevelt's office. After the preliminaries, he said, "There's not much except to confirm that Amelia Earhart was here on 21 December 1936. Mrs. Roosevelt escorted her into the Oval Office at three in the afternoon to meet President Roosevelt. The President's steward served pekoe tea, a variety of cookies, and square-cut cucumber sandwiches. The meeting adjourned at four o'clock. That's all there is."

Concerned, I asked, "There ought to be more. What did they discuss?"

With a shrug of his shoulders, Roosevelt responded, "I don't know. There's no record of any discussions."

Incredulous that the official record was so deficient, I spouted, "That doesn't make sense. White House records are always completely detailed. There has to be more."

"Perhaps, but there's nothing more in the official record."

"What about unofficial records?" I cracked with a touch of annoyance.

Trying to smooth troubled waters, Roosevelt offered, "Commander, there are no unofficial records about Miss Earhart's visit."

"Have you asked the President?"

"No. He has been in conference with General Marshall, Admiral King, and their staffs since yesterday. There's no need. If I were to ask him, his response would be 'Who?.'"

Defeated, I rose to leave. As a last-gasp query, I asked, "Was anyone else present?"

"There is an ink notation, 'Other guests were present.'"

"What guests? What were their names?"

"Commander, I've told you everything that's in the record. I cannot help you further."

I rose and thanked him for his cooperation.

The Attendees

In a somewhat frustrated mode, I returned to my office and discussed the White House visit with my Intelligence Yeoman, Donald Pickart, a bright young man from Mule Shoe, Texas. "There were others in that meeting with Earhart. Who? Why?" I propped my feet on the desk, leaned back in my chair, closed my eyes, and let my mind wander. *We can crack this mystery of the 'other guests' with logic and initiative.* "Pickart, let's prepare a list of possible candidates and then find out where they were at 1500 hours on 21 December 1936."

Finding out who had attended the Earhart meeting was not overly complicated. We used a three-pronged probe. We asked each targeted person's secretary or aide to check the daily calendar for that time and date. If that drew a blank, we got copies of their daily automobile-trip records. Lastly, we checked the White House's gate log. Two weeks later, we had a list of the most likely candidates—most were confirmed one hundred percent and the few others ninety-five percent confirmed. They were senior officers in the Navy, State, and War Departments, the director of the Civil Aeronautics Board, and the president of Pan American World Airways. No need to name these folks now, I'll discuss them in my concluding section.

Confirming that Earhart had met with the President and learning who else had been present was a central step in my research. But where would I find the next clue? I was stumped.

Yeoman Pickart thought for a few moments and said, "Go to Honolulu and check out the files at CINCPACFLT (Commander-in-Chief Pacific Fleet), and even the public library. Never know what you'll find."

CINCPACFLT, Pearl Harbor

A few days later, after a trans-Pacific flight on a China Clipper, I was at CINCPACFLT*, Makalapa, Pearl Harbor, perusing the files at the Fleet Intelligence Center. After three days, I had found nothing of import related to Earhart's flight—a few scraps of miscellaneous information that by now was public information. I expressed my frustration to the Security Chief Petty Officer. He empathized with me and said he could offer no more help. "There are no other Naval Intelligence records in Hawaii." I was at another dead end.

I refused to concede. After a few seconds I asked him, "What about Station Hypo* files?"

Frowning, he replied, "That's an operation that I have no knowledge of or access to."

"Is that operation located in this building?"

"I have no idea," he replied forcefully.

With unease, he replied in a soft voice, "Go down that ladder (stairs), turn right, walk the passageway about one hundred steps, find the green door, push the red buzzer next to the door, and stand by."

That's exactly what I did. Shortly, a small peephole opened in the door and I heard a booming voice over a hidden loudspeaker.

"State your name and business."

"I am Commander Richard Gregory from the Director of Naval Intelligence Office, and I do not have the prerogative to discuss my business in this passageway."

There was a long pause. The voice boomed again, "You do not have the appropriate clearance to enter these spaces. Permission denied."

Clearly, I had been summarily dismissed. I pressed the buzzer three times.

The voice said, "You have no business here."

I shouted quickly, "I am on essential business for the DNI. I must speak with Commander Rochford."

"Stand by."

A couple of minutes later the door opened about halfway and the voice said, "Enter. Do exactly what you are told. If you do not, the consequences are dire." I entered a small room, bare of everything. The outer door closed. A sailor entered, dressed in the tropical white uniform—no rating badge or insignia of any kind was on his uniform. Around his waist was a guard belt carrying a Colt 45 in a leather holster. He was followed by a six-foot-tall Marine with his Thompson submachine gun at the ready position. *Egad! What rabbit hole am I in?*

The sailor spoke softly and respectfully, "Commander, do not speak to anyone, do not touch anything, do nothing to cause this Marine alarm. Understand?"

"Indeed, I do."

"I must put this blindfold on you."

With that task accomplished, he led me a few short steps to Rochford's office.

A new voice said, "I am the Executive Officer of Station Hypo. What is your business?"

Clearly, this was a no-nonsense operation. I got to the point. "I represent the DNI and I am working to discover exactly what Amelia Earhart's mission was in 1937 and what happened to her. Does this outfit have any information on her last flight?"

"Interesting." There was a long pause, silent except for that harmonious buzz in the background. Three or four minutes later the voice said, "We have no Earhart information for you. Good day."

And, that's that. Another bust and nowhere to go.

I advanced to the Officer's Club to partake in adult beverages at Happy Hour. After a while, my frustration eased as the bourbon flowed. Later, as I lay in my bunk with the 'world spinning 'round in my head,' I had another last-ditch, what-the-hell notion.

Honolulu State Library

Around noon, I had recovered enough to navigate the stairs to the Honolulu State Library*. I dressed in mufti to allay any concerns about a naval officer asking about old-time photographs. The head librarian, a charming, grandmotherly woman, led me to their photographic archives and asked an assistant librarian to help me. Going through the index cards, we found several files of photographs of the Islands dated in the 1930s. Several files contained Earhart photographs. None were relevant to my research. Another file caught my interest, one labeled "Miscellaneous Photographs." And that's exactly what they were—miscellaneous and of no interest. The assistant librarian recalled that some of the older photographs were stored in one of the city's warehouses, but she did not know which one.

Not to be deterred, I spent several days working with city officials and searching far too many warehouse files without success. Then, I was told by an old-timer in the Maintenance Department that he'd seen some ancient file cabinets labeled "State Library Photographs" in Warehouse Number 7-J at the north end of the island.

"If you get an automobile, I'll show you," the fellow offered.

That afternoon we arrived at a city complex of several dozen warehouses. The old-timer popped the lock on Warehouse 7-J with a key on his massive key ring, and led me to a storeroom of automotive parts. In the file-cabinet section for maintenance records, we found several library file cabinets labeled "Miscellaneous Photographs." My companion had no idea how the cabinets got there or why, nor what to do with them. To him they were just part of the scenery, and someone else's concern.

In the top drawer of one of the rusted cabinets, I found three heavy-duty, expandable wallets bound together with several wraps of thick brown string. On the outward-facing wallet was a hand-scribbled notation in large black letters, "No interest. Return to Sender." The tingle returned with a vengeance. *What sender?* I cut the string and ripped open the first wallet. There they were! Nine-inch by nine-inch, black-and-white, stereo-pair photographs stamped "TOP SECRET MERCURY." I shouted, "Bingo squared!"

My escort looked at me with concern but did not speak.

Hand-printed on each photograph were the initials "A.E.," the name "Truk," and the date "01 July 1937." *Success! At long last.* I shook vigorously my escort's hand and shouted, "Thanks. Thanks, a million."

In all, I recovered 80 stereo pairs. I scanned these aerial photographs* quickly and saw a host of military targets: airfields with scores of aircraft, anti-aircraft batteries, coastal defense emplacements, harbor installations, dry docks, wharfs, floating cranes, warehouses, petrol storage areas, power plants, and military barracks. In the harbor were warships of all classes, including submarines, troopships, and utility ships—a treasure trove of A-1 intelligence. I was elated at my find, and yet deeply disturbed that this compartmented intelligence information was stored so cavalierly. Nonetheless, I had the photographs and that is what counted.

I rode shotgun as we returned to Honolulu. I clasped the rebound wallets close to my chest. My mind was whirling. Earhart had done it! *Nice going, ol' girl!* Amelia Earhart photographed Truk, the Empire of Japan's most secret and largest military installation in Micronesia, the "Gibraltar of the Pacific." My mind whirled with the implications of this treasure trove of intelligence. *You done good, Amelia Earhart, as we Texans are apt to say.*

Again, I could not escape the troubling question: why and how was such highly classified intelligence left in the open? And, what photographic laboratory processed this top-secret film and left it unsecured? Without much reflection, the answer became obvious: a Hughes Tool Corporation photographic laboratory secreted in these islands. On reflection, I concluded that at this late date it did not matter. I had Earhart's aerial photographs of Truk.

Photographic Interpretation

A few days later, I was back in my office at Naval Intelligence Headquarters. Pickart and I scanned the photographs. They were exceptionally sharp, the contrast and exposure were on target, and the shadow detail was excellent. (For the professional photographer: the Dmax and the Dmin were optimum.) The photographs were exceptionally clean: no streaks, no fog, and no spots. The laboratory that processed and printed that aerial film was first class—from a Hughes operation, I would expect no less.

Our first task was to do some basic photography metrics. We computed the scale of the photographs and determined that with the 24-inch lens, at this scale, Earhart was at 9,637 feet, and was straight and level when she activated the Fairchild camera. Pickart calculated that Earhart was flying at about 100 knots as she started her photographic run—necessary to get thirty percent overlapping stereo coverage at this altitude and the camera's recycle rate. The folks at the Hughes Tool hangar in Alameda did a superb job of calculating and adjusting the camera's functions at its installation.

After completing the photographic run, she had shut off the camera, advanced the throttles to boost the Electra to its normal cruising speed or perhaps somewhat faster, changed her heading to a southeasterly course toward Howland, climbed to a higher altitude, and exited Japanese air space. The Electra faded into the darkening sky. I doubt that the Japanese knew she had penetrated their Bamboo Curtain and overflown Truk.

The admiral smiled ear to ear as he reviewed the Earhart photographs. He used Pickart's stereoscope viewfinder to study each of the stereo pairs in a three-dimensional view. Whenever he spotted something of interest, he issued a small grunt. Finished, he carefully rearranged the photographs in sequence, tapped them on his desk to straighten them, put them in his briefcase, looked at me, and said, "Fine job, Commander. Take a few days off."

Final Logbook

In this concluding section, I owe it to you, dear reader, to chronicle my interpretation of the events surrounding Amelia Earhart's disappearance—the final logbook entry for her last flight, as it were.

To set the perspective for our government's involvement in Earhart's flight, I will recreate that 21 December 1936 meeting in the White House as if I were there and recording the proceedings in real time. I've built this scene from interviews with the remaining attendees, perusing the official logbooks of the attendees, and adding my educated speculation.

The White House

On 21 December 1936, about 1500 hours, Eleanor Roosevelt* escorted Amelia Earhart, her friend, into the Oval Office and introduced her to President Roosevelt. With his biggest smile and with his cigarette holder held at that jaunty angle, the President greeted her. "Welcome, Miss Earhart. We're delighted that you've come to the Oval Office to discuss your proposed around-the-world flight. Come, sit by my desk."

Earhart approached the President and shook his hand, "Thank you, Mister President. I am delighted to meet you."

"Eleanor has told me about your career, and I am impressed by your accomplishments."

"Mister President, please skip that Miss title. Amelia or Earhart is just fine." As she sat, she glanced around the room and saw a cadre of official-looking persons. *Who are these fellows and what are they doing here?* She spotted Eugene (Gene) Vidal*, and tried to suppress a serious frown, unsuccessfully. Vidal is her current paramour.

With a smile in his voice the President answered, "That's okay with me." He paused and changed his gaze to the others in the room. "First, meet these associates of mine. I've asked these fellows to attend this meeting so that we'll know best how to help you in your upcoming around-the-world flight." He made the introductions, jabbing his cigarette holder at each person in turn. He paused at Vidal and commented, with a hint of naughty in his voice, "Of course, you already know Mister Vidal, our Director of the Civil Aeronautics Board."

Somewhat bewildered at the august company in the room and somewhat miffed at the President's *vilaine fille* hint, Earhart nonetheless acknowledged them with, "My pleasure, gentlemen."

At a secret signal, a Filipino steward entered and served tea and snacks. The President commented, "May I offer you anything, Amelia?"

"A glass of iced tea, please."

Several minutes later her glass was empty.

"What else may I offer you?"

"Nothing, thank you, sir. I'm fine." She forced a nervous smile. "Shall I discuss my flight?"

"Shortly, Amelia." Roosevelt took a long drag on his cigarette, exhaled, and let the smoke drift lazily upward and away. "You are a loyal American, I assume? And want the best for our country?"

His blunt question caused apprehension to grip her face. Earhart responded with a quick snap, "Absolutely. I have always expounded the virtues of my country." She paused and took a quick glance around the room. "May I ask why these senior officials in your administration are here? I thought we were going to have a private meeting to get acquainted and for me to tell you about the plans for the around-the-world flight."

"In a few minutes, I'll explain. If Eleanor misled you, I apologize. She has a subtle way of inveigling people to her will. We invited you to the Oval Office because I want to ask a favor of you." He paused for a few seconds to let his comment register. "From this point forward, everything said and seen in this room is confidential. Are you comfortable with that proscription, Amelia?"

With questioning eyes, she responded haltingly, "May I ask why?"

"Not yet, Amelia. Will you keep this meeting to yourself—speak of it to no one? Not even your husband."

Realizing that if she does not agree, the meeting would be over and the Roosevelt administration would not assist in her flight, Earhart replied with a hint of agitation, "Yes, sir." She squirmed in her chair and blurted out, "Absolutely, I will."

"All right." Roosevelt points his cigarette holder at Cordell Hull*, the Secretary of State. "Fill in our guest on some of the details in Europe."

"Thank you, Mister President." Secretary Hull looked directly at Earhart and spoke in a clear, authoritative voice.

"The State Department's Bureau of Intelligence and Research tells me that the Third Reich*, Nazi Germany, will start a war in Europe in a few years—a repeat of the Great War but with more scope, vengeance, and destruction. Even though we'll be officially neutral, we'll help the Allies secretly—but everyone will know of it. There's no doubt that sooner or later we'll be in the thick of it."

Puzzled, Earhart responded, "I haven't paid much attention to what's happening in Europe. I'm consumed with my flying, publicity activities, and marketing business."

"Please understand, to all intents and purposes, that the Second World War has already begun. Nazi Germany's official foreign policy is *Lebensraum*—taking territory from her neighbors for German living space and to make Germany self-sufficient in food and raw materials. Earlier this year, the Nazis occupied the Rhineland in violation of the Treaty of Versailles. We have intelligence that their next move is to occupy Austria and then the Sudetenland region of Czechoslovakia. Their burgeoning Luftwaffe's Condor Legion* is fighting in the Spanish Civil War, supporting General Franco's army against the Comintern's* Republican government. Benito Mussolini's* fascist army has captured Cyrenaica and Abyssinia and have illegally occupied Corfu, and will soon conquer Albania."

Wondering why Secretary Hull was telling her about these European problems, Earhart responded with a hint of disinterest. "I suppose I've heard some of these things on the radio but paid no attention. My focus was elsewhere. Your narrative sounds ominous."

In his most serious voice Hull continued, "It's much more ominous, Earhart. In the Orient, warlords, the Spirit Warriors, dominate the government of the Empire of Japan. In 1931, their Kwangtung Army* invaded and occupied the Chinese province of Manchuria, making it their puppet state and dubbing it Manchukuo. The Army then took control of the Chinese section of the Trans-Siberian Railroad. Japanese patrols reconnoiter Inner Mongolia and Sinkiang Provinces, and fight with the Communist Eight Army and Nationalist Army units. The Kwangtung Army clashes frequently with Mongolian cavalry and Soviet army patrols—sometimes the fighting is intense and casualties on both sides are high."

Hull paused to gather his thoughts.

"We believe Japan's goal is to control all of East Asia and the Pacific to the edge of the Territory of Hawaii—and perhaps including it. We reckon that the warlords are planning a Pacific war to eliminate all Occidental influence in the area."

Bewildered by what Secretary Hull has said, Earhart responded, "I don't understand, Secretary Hull. Japan was our ally in the Great War. In 1923, we sent tons and tons of aid to them at the time of the great earthquake. I can't imagine what you're saying!" She fretted and looked about the room as if someone would explain. She blurted, "Why are you telling me this confidential information?"

The President jabbed his cigarette holder toward Captain Hayne Ellis, USN, Director of the Office of Naval Intelligence. "Captain, brief Earhart on our Pacific dilemma."

Captain Ellis stood and looked around the room, mentally checking everyone present. "Thank you, Mister President." Facing Earhart, he began in a stern voice, "Miss Earhart, before I continue I must ask if you are willing to swear a sacred oath of secrecy regarding a highly-classified intelligence program. Only those people with a strict need to know are privy to information about this program. If you agree, you are bound by this oath until the Director of Naval Intelligence or the President releases you from it. If you refuse, there will be no ill will. We will wish you *bon voyage* on your flight and we'll say no more. Of course, all that you've seen and heard today is confidential, and you are forbidden to mention it to anyone. Is all that clear?"

Earhart gasped at this request. She put her right hand to her mouth. In a few seconds, she dropped her hand and rubbed her left forearm. Her mind was whirling at what the Naval Intelligence captain was proposing. *What are these people doing to me?* She looked at the President and sputtered, "What you're asking is outside my ken. I have no comprehension or experience in naval intelligence and covert activities. I must know why you're asking me to take this oath. What is this favor you want of me?"

Henry L. Woodring*, Secretary of War, interjected, "Earhart, we need your help. It's that simple. It's a matter of grave importance to our nation, and you are uniquely qualified to help your country. Do you need more time, Earhart? Perhaps a glass of wine?"

"No. No. I'm okay. May I have time to consider?" Without waiting for an answer, she closed her eyes. In a few seconds, she opened them and turned to the President. "I'm in an untenable position. You haven't explained this favor you want from me. How can I make such a momentous decision when I don't know the ground rules?" With growing frustration she exploded, "And what are Gene Vidal and Juan Trippe* doing here? What's their interest in this secret business?"

The President did not respond, nor did anyone else. Earhart realized that her entreaty would not be answered. She slumped in her chair and closed her eyes.

An indulgent silence pervaded the room. After a couple of minutes, Admiral William Standley, USN, Commander in Chief of the United States Fleet, spoke in a voice that was almost a purr. "Amelia, before you make your decision, I am obligated to caution you that if you accept the oath and agree to the President's favor, there will be serious risks—severe enough that your life may be sacrificed."

Earhart popped out of her chair. "You're going to make me spy! That's it, isn't it? That's what this whole damn charade is about. Isn't it?"

Admiral Standley responded, "In a way you're correct, but perhaps not in the way you envision. We cannot continue this discussion without your decision."

Earhart looked at him, and started to speak. But did not. She buried her head in her hands to ease the torment. A deathly silence pervaded the Oval Office. If someone had listened very closely, a quiet snuffle could have been heard.

The President broke the silence in his most persuasive voice, "Amelia, we'll not kowtow to the warlords of the Rising Sun. Your acceptance will mean saving the lives of thousands of American sailors and soldiers. I empathize with your frustration. But, you're the only option we have. Take all the time you need to decide."

Earhart soon sat upright in her chair and turned to Admiral Standley. "What the hell! Sure, I'll do it. At heart, I'm a risk taker. I take a risk every time I fly."

Captain Ellis approached Earhart and handed her a bible. "Please stand, Amelia Earhart Putnam. Put your right hand on this King James Bible." On cue, all others stood, except for the President, bound to his wheelchair. The captain administered the oath and Earhart swore compliance. "Congratulations, Amelia Earhart, you are now authorized to receive compartmented intelligence that is classified Top Secret, code word MERCURY. Please return to your chair. We have a lot to discuss."

"Yes, Captain. Thank you." She sat and stared with narrowed eyes at Trippe and Vidal, again wondering why these two important men were included in this top-secret program.

Captain Ellis noticed Earhart's quizzical expression. "I see your concern, Earhart. I briefed Messieurs Vidal and Trippe into the MERCURY program some time ago. They will help you fulfill the President's request. First, however, I must caution you not to mention to anyone that you are in this program or even mention its name. Such information is classified at the same high security level as information in the MERCURY program. Later, you'll be briefed on the personnel in this program whom you must know in order to complete your task. Do you have any questions?"

"No. No, sir. Not now."

"Very well." Captain Ellis snapped as if responding to a junior officer.

In a matter-of-fact voice he continued, "Earhart, here's the background." He told her about the Japanese takeover of Micronesia, the Bamboo Curtain, and their suspected fortifications of the islands. "We have reason to believe they're building a large naval base at Truk in the Caroline Islands. From this base, the Japanese will launch a war in the Pacific on the British, Dutch, French, and the United States of America."

Claude Swanson*, Secretary of the Navy, sat forward and spoke. "We have almost no intelligence on the Japanese fortifications in Micronesia. Without it, we're at a serious disadvantage, and when the Japanese attack our peacetime Navy, we'll take a beating. In just a few weeks, the Japanese Navy could well be on our California coast and with the Rising Sun flag flying over Pearl Harbor."

The President interjected, "Amelia, it's that serious." He paused for effect. "We want you to take aerial photographs of the Japanese naval base at Truk in the Carolines."

Earhart gasped and sat stiffly upright. She looked about the room as if seeking solace. There was none. She closed her eyes, dropped her head, and said nothing. A discreet silence imbued the Oval Office. She looked at President Roosevelt. "May I have a shot of bourbon? Straight." One gulp and her glass was empty. In a resigned voice, she addressed the room, "Okay. You got a deal. I'll do it! Sure, I'll do it." In a mocking voce she exclaimed, "I've always wanted to be a Mata Hari. What other surprises have you for me?"

Captain Ellis responded in kind, "None for now, Amelia Earhart."

Without a 'thank you,' the President and Mrs. Roosevelt excused themselves and retired. Secretary Woodring, Secretary Swanson, and Admiral Standley also departed, with appropriate ado. Then, Secretary Hull addressed Earhart. "The State Department is working with Gene Vidal's Civil Aeronautics Board, which is the lead agency in obtaining over-flight permissions, visas, and any other international action that you'll need. Vidal will work with you on flight details, and he'll be your primary contact dealing with foreign relations in this project. Now, please excuse me. I have another meeting to attend."

Admiral Standley stood and shook Earhart's hand. He said, "Thank you, Amelia Earhart. We're counting on your success, and the Navy is going to do all in our power to make it happen. For starters, we're going to build an airstrip on Howland Island. The Navy will need it when the next war starts. Additionally, we'll have fuel and oil products, and other supplies, stationed on Howland for your final two legs. We're going to move Polynesian laborers to Howland to do the work, maintain the place, and ward off intruders."

Standley continued, "We'll have a security-cleared contractor install our latest radio direction-finder in your Electra." He watched for her reaction. He knew full well that Earhart had refused repeatedly Paul Mantz's entreaties to teach her the operating procedure for the direction-finder.

Earhart mumbled some sort of nonplussed response.

He continued. "I'll have three ships on stations to assist you: the Coast Guard cutter *Itasca* on Howland as your guard ship, the Coast Guard cutter *Ontario* just south of Nauru in the British Mandated Ellis Islands, and the minesweeper *USS Swan* midway between Howland and Hawaii. These ships will help guide you on your course and update weather information, and the *Itasca* will send strong radio signals for your direction-finder to guide you toward Howland. Captain Ellis will be your contact for naval affairs."

Standley paused for emphasis. "Earhart, I must caution you that Japanese intelligence will monitor your radio transmissions. Accordingly, no matter the reason, you must maintain absolute radio silence after you turn north from Lae en route to Truk, and until you are about an hour back on your original great-circle route to Howland. When you broadcast again, send a false flag signal—a ruse as it were. Report that Noonan found the problem and fixed it."

Admiral Standley moved close to Earhart. He placed his hand on her shoulder and looked straight into her eyes. "Miss Earhart, you've volunteered for a dangerous mission. I must warn you, should the Japanese capture you, we will deny knowing you. You will be on your own, and you'll face some incredibly difficult times." He dropped to one knee so that they were face to face. "Amelia, our agent at Lae will offer you a tablet. It's deadly. Consider if you would use it in the event of imminent capture." He rose. "No one can resist the. Kenepitai's* interrogation for very long and a sure death awaits—frequently a slow and painful one for spies."

Earhart stared at the Admiral and her eyes narrowed. After a few seconds she responded, "I understand."

"Excellent."

Juan Trippe commented, "Earhart, please know that Pan American World Airways will provide full cooperation on your around-the-world flight. Pan American's radio stations throughout the Pacific will monitor your radio transmissions and relay messages via the *Ontario* and the *Itasca*. We'll provide radio checks and weather information, and monitor your progress. And, I'll have one of our Clipper ships on standby ready to scramble in an emergency. Now, I must leave with Admiral Standley." He handed her his card, which listed his on-desk and operator telephone numbers. "Call me any time, night or day."

A Marine master sergeant in firmly-pressed dress blues appeared and escorted Earhart, Vidal, and Captain Ellis to a room deep under the White House. A steward entered and asked how he could be of service—lemonade and roast beef sandwiches perhaps? He returned shortly with their requests.

Refreshed, Earhart asked Captain Ellis, "Pray tell, how am I to accomplish this aerial reconnaissance mission? I'm completely out of my element."

Ellis answered, "My staff has developed an Operation Plan that details all facets of this venture. In the days following, we'll fill in the details."

Earhart snapped, "You fellows have worked an excellent con job on me." She cracked a slow smile. "You knew from the beginning that I would agree. Nice goin'."

Ellis smiled broadly. "We probably know you better than you know yourself." He rolled out a very small-scale chart of the central Pacific on a large oak table. "Let's get to business." Using the chart as his focus, he outlined his Operation Plan's strategy for the fundamentals of her assignment.

In conclusion, he said, "My staff will explore the technical details with you in the next several days."

Puzzled, Earhart queried, "What about Fred Noonan, my navigator? His input is integral to my flight, and he has to know about this reconnaissance plan."

"Reserve Lieutenant Commander Fred Noonan is a Naval Intelligence officer and is briefed in another intelligence program. He'll be here tomorrow, and we'll swear him into the MERCURY program."

Earhart was staggered by this astonishing information. But, on reflection, she did not express any surprise. Calmly she mocked, "I should have expected something like that."

For the next few days Earhart, Vidal, Noonan, and various Naval Intelligence and aviation personnel were in seclusion at Camp David working out the fine details of her flight into Micronesia: courses, altitude, air speed, ground speed, initial point, exit point, easterly winds, projected weather in July, and a myriad other details.

See Figure # 5 for a map of Earhart's Modified Course.

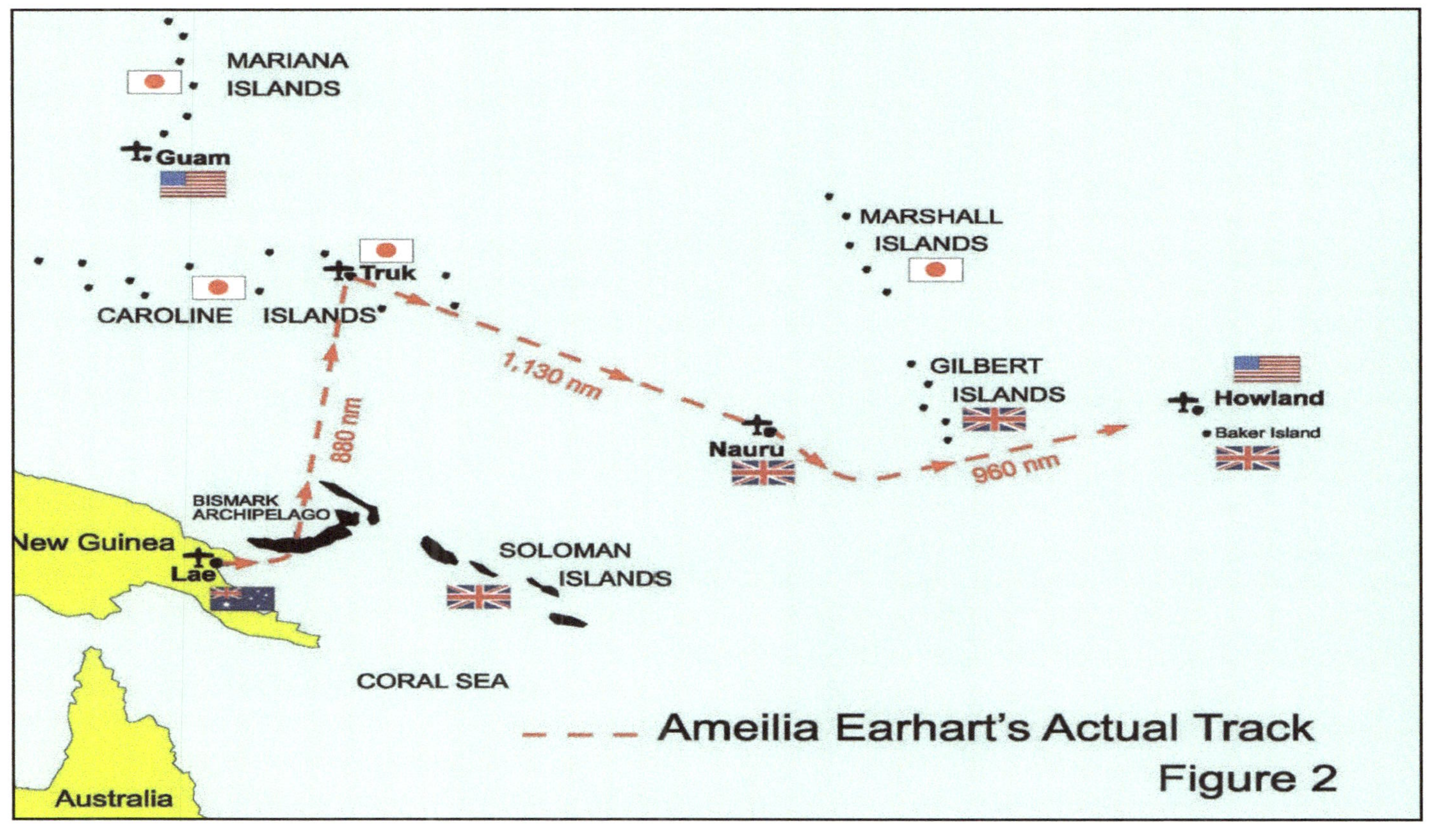

Figure 5. Earhart's Modified Course

Toward the end of these briefings, Chief Petty Officer Munoz told Earhart, "Clearly, the Japanese have a command and control early warning system. Their aircraft defenses will consist of antiaircraft guns* and interceptor aircraft*. We've no intelligence about Truk's air defenses—their number, emplacement, or quality. Nonetheless, they must be formidable. Should their intercepts of your radio signals arouse suspicion, air defense command will order a continuous combat air patrol—the CAP—for a radius of about 100 kilometer from the atoll. If you are detected, they'll vector the CAP for an intercept and scramble every asset they have to bring you down. If they are flying some of their older aircraft, and you spot them soon enough, you probably could outrun them."

Earhart cracked that slow smile of hers. "Thanks a million, Chief. Just what I needed to know." She paused for a moment. "What if those Nippers are flying their newer aircraft and fire machine guns at me? Got any surefire advice?"

"None. But a suggestion." He looks at the map and blinks his eyes several times to clear his mind. With the most authentic voice he can muster, he continues, "If you are air intercepted or experience anti-aircraft fire, fly a zig-zag course as fast as possible and exit Japanese air space *très vite.*"

"Abandon my mission?"

"Your decision madam."

In a slightly mocking voice, Earhart responded, "Chief Munoz, you're a sweetheart. Anything else?"

Not skipping a beat, Munoz continued, "On completion of your photographic run, bank hard to the right, crank those Wasp engines to max power, climb as high as you are able, and head southeast."

"I can do that." She paused for sarcastic effect. "If my Electra and *moi* are not critically hurt."

Without responding, Munoz continued, "I reckon that at 10,000 feet, the Nippers probably will not know that you are overflying their primary naval base in Micronesia."

Camera Installation

In this concluding section, I offer my hypothesis on how the Navy prepared Earhart's Electra for her aerial reconnaissance mission and what happened during the final couple days of her last flight.

Sometime around midnight on 19 May 1937, Amelia Earhart*, piloting her Electra, took off from the Lockheed facility at Burbank Airport in California. Her VFR flight-plan's destination was the Oakland airport, her home base. About 200 miles out, she changed course and swung the Electra over San Francisco Bay. In a few minutes, she approached the Naval Air Station in Alameda to make an unnoticed and unofficial landing. As Naval Intelligence had instructed, she made no radio request for landing instructions. On her down-wind leg, she flashed her landing lights twice in quick succession, and three seconds later she flashed the lights one more time. The solitary Air Control man* in the Alameda tower used an ALDIS light gun to signal a flashing green light, communicating that she was cleared to approach the air station. On her base leg, he signaled a steady green light, meaning that she was cleared to land.

The Electra touched down. After it completed its roll, a man in civilian clothes appeared. He used a hand-held, yellow-light wand to direct the Electra to a darkened hangar on the east side of the field. Earhart taxied her Electra toward it. As she approached, the hangar's twin doors slid open and bright light flooded the area. A man in civilian clothes gave her the 'cut engines' hand signal. Immediately after the engine's last cough, several men attached a tow bar to the Electra and a cart pulled the airplane inside. The hangar doors slid closed silently. The entire approach and landing operation took less than four minutes.

Another civilian helped Earhart deplane and escorted her to a lush waiting room. A young woman of Oriental descent, dressed in a skintight cheongsam, greeted her and said with a barely noticeable accent, "My name is Yen. I am here to help you. I would suggest that the lounge chair is most comfortable. May I offer you refreshments: tea, coffee, whiskey, champagne, chocolates? How may I serve you?"

Somewhat bemused by the opulence of the place and the dutiful service, Earhart said uneasily, "Ice water will be fine."

Inside, the aerial camera installation proceeded apace. A former Navy Aviation Machinist Mate pulled out the copilot's seat and controls, and cut a four-inch by four-inch hole in the Electra's skin next to parallel spars below the copilot's station. From underneath the aircraft, he drilled four screw-holes into the spars at the corners of the hole. With the help of an ex-Navy Photographer's Mate, they bolted the KA-17 camera in place. The photographer attached the magazine, now pre-loaded with the nine-inch Aero-Plus X film, set the camera's shutter speed at 1/250 second and the lens at f8.0, and attached the starburst K2 filter over the lens. To activate the camera's motor, he rigged a power cable to carry twenty-eight volts DC to the camera magazine, and secured it to a small stanchion close to Earhart's right hand. He set the recycle speed at 1.0 seconds—the correct speed for thirty percent overlap at the Electra's preplanned speed and altitude over the target. On completion, the photographer made a thorough installation inspection, then started the magazine's motor, to cycle a few frames of film and ensure that the aerial-camera suite was functioning properly. Meanwhile, below the Electra, the machinist covered the square opening with a prefabricated, aluminum cover plate with quick-release screws.

Their supervisor, Sydney J. Kellogg, checked and rechecked the Fairchild KA-17 camera suite operation and installation. Satisfied that it was functioning properly, he told the two men, "Okay. Fine job."

Several hours later, a messenger brought Earhart to the Electra. The photographer briefed her on procedures to withdraw and install the magazine's dark slide, activate the magazine's motor, remove the magazine from the camera, and stow it in its case. Earhart practiced the procedure a few times. After her third successful operation, the fellow acknowledged her competence with the "thumbs up" hand signal. He covered the camera suite with a fitted black tarpaulin. Stenciled in large, bright white letters atop the cover and on two sides were the warnings, "Delicate Instruments. DO NOT TOUCH."

Underneath the Electra, he showed Earhart how to work the quick-release screws to remove the aluminum cover plate.

The aviatrix gave a hearty, "I understand."

The photographer spoke in sotto voce, "On landing on Howland, a Hughes Tool crew will remove the camera, install the control column and seat, and replace the plate." Without adieu, he left the area.

Earhart said to the fading silhouette of the fellow, "I'm impressed with your professionalism. Thanks."

Unidentified civilians made other modifications to the Electra. Because there is no documentation, I don't know what these fellows did to the Electra. Nonetheless, I speculate that they beefed up the Pratt & Whitney Wasp engines to boost their horsepower and increase the Electra's speed. Meanwhile, back in the lounge, a Naval Intelligence commander whom Earhart had met at Camp David administered the oath of office to her and commissioned her a Lieutenant in the Naval Reserve.

The Flight

In the early morning hours at Lae, Earhart conducted her walk-around, pre-flight check of the Electra. All was well. She removed the aluminum cover plate from the camera port. In the cockpit she withdrew the dark slide from the film magazine and stowed it in a leather pocket on the bulkhead behind her.

One of the Australian station employees brought lunch bags and canteens of water to the flyers. As he handed the lunch bag to Earhart he whispered, "It's in the yellow box."

She glanced at Noonan.

He nodded in the affirmative.

Earhart accepted the lunch bag and said, quietly, "Thank you."

On 1 July 1937, at 1000 hours, Earhart gunned the Wasp engines on the heavily-laden Electra*. After an inordinate long run, the aircraft lifted from the runway, and headed toward Howland Island—2,333 nautical miles east. During her climb to cruising altitude, 9,000 feet, she flew on her projected great-circle route. Over the following hour, she transmitted several routine radio messages. About 1100 hours, she banked her Electra eighty degrees to the left, climbed to 10,000 feet, and set a course for Truk Atoll, inside the Bamboo Curtain, a course Noonan had carefully computed. Hours later, Earhart spotted Truk Atoll in the near distance, dead ahead. The low-angle afternoon sun had cast telltale shadows on the targets, making them stand out: easier for photographic interpreters to spot, identify, and measure.

As Earhart approached the initial point, she searched for Japanese aircraft—none in sight. She reduced the Electra's true airspeed to 105 knots. When she reached the initial point, she flicked the magazine motor to ON. The blinking green light on the magazine told her that the camera suite was working properly. She tensed apprehensively, waiting for the black smoke puff of exploding anti-aircraft shells to appear. Nonetheless, she held a steady course and altitude. The Electra was over the target for about three minutes. No black puffs appeared. And no machine-gun bullets ripped the Electra.

Clearing the harbor, Earhart switched the magazine motor OFF, executed Chief Munoz's instructions, and vanished into the closing darkness. If the Japanese were aware of Amelia Earhart's penetration of their Bamboo Curtain, we have no evidence of it.

Finale

Most pundits aver that Earhart crashed into the Pacific somewhere near Howland and that she and Noonan perished. If that is so, then the overriding question is, how did the Navy get the photographs from the aerial camera? For a fact, I do not know.

I'll propose a plausible scenario. Earlier, while cruising en route to Howland, Earhart slid the dark slide into the film magazine, uncoupled it, stowed it in its case, and passed the case over the in-cabin fuel tanks to Noonan's waiting hands. Shortly afterward, she changed to a new heading, one that Chief Munoz had computed. Several hours later she began her let-down and made her approach to the small airfield on Nauru Island* in the British Mandated Ellis Islands, closed at this time of night.

Earhart turned on the Electra's landing lights as she began the final approach. Activated by a photo-electric device, the runway lights lit brightly, outlining both edges of the strip. After touchdown and roll-out, Earhart kept the Electra's engines ticking. Noonan popped open the cabin door. A man in mufti scampered to the Electra. He verified his credentials as a U.S. Naval Intelligence officer by uttering a phrase only the flyers and he knew. Noonan handed him the film magazine, slammed the door shut, and locked it. Earhart gunned the engines and the Electra leaped into the night and faded away. On climb-out, Earhart noticed a Pan American China Clipper secured to a wharf on the leeward side of the island.

You may well ask, "Why did Earhart land on Nauru when she was scheduled to land on Howland and transfer the film magazine there?" We'll never know the exact reason. My supposition is that Paul Mantz alerted Captain Ellis to Earhart's meager radio skills and maladroit operation of the radio direction-finder. These deficiencies and unknown weather extant in mid-July in the area significantly decreased Earhart's odds of finding Howland—a dot in the vast central Pacific about 1,000 nautical miles distant. Ellis decided to take no chance of losing those priceless aerial photographs.

Captain Ellis chose British Nauru because it would be significantly easier to find than Howland. It was much closer to Truk, and it lay only 200 nautical miles northwest of her projected great-circle route. Nauru was much larger, better populated, and well lighted. From its two radio stations, powerful long- and short-wave radio transmissions were broadcast continuously. If Earhart was marginally competent, she could use her Bendix radio direction-finder to follow these powerful electronic signals guiding her to the island. As it were, I reckon it was Noonan's celestial navigation skills that vectored Earhart to Nauru.

From Nauru's "International Notice to Airmen," Ellis knew that, late at night, the airport was closed and the control tower unmanned. The rotating beacon on the control tower remained lit twenty-four hours a day to accommodate aircraft emergencies. This beacon emitted a strong, alternating white and green light set at fifteen degrees above the horizon.

Our intelligence officer entered Nauru as a crew member on that Pan American China Clipper ship. The captain must have declared some kind of in-flight emergency to explain this unscheduled and off-course landing at Nauru.

That's my most likely interpretation of Amelia Earhart's last flight.

You may wonder why, for this complicated scenario involving so many people, there are no records or photographs. In the intelligence business, it's routine not to record such clandestine events or else to destroy all evidence quickly.

Epilogue

Nota bene. My father, Captain Richard Gregory, USN, was killed in action when a Japanese kamikaze slammed into the aircraft carrier *USS Franklin***** on 19 March 1945. My dad was the staff air-intelligence officer for Admiral Marc Mitchner's Task Force 58.

Signed
Randolph Gregory, Ensign. USN

What Happened to Amelia Earhart?

To date, there is not a scintilla of hard, verifiable evidence that would confirm the facts of Earhart's disappearance. Her fate, and that of her navigator Fred Noonan, and the Lockheed Electra, is an enigma that endures to a fare-thee-well in aviation lore. Where the aviatrix disappeared and what happened are the two key questions that are unanswerable with the information we have today. We do not know.

Notwithstanding these facts, over the years, a gaggle of pundits have posited numerous scenarios that endeavor to explain her last flight. Several are based on the physical science and posit intriguing answers. Others promulgate scenarios based on apocryphal information and wishful imagination. Others are so outlandish as to be dismissed out of hand. For example, the proposition that the Japanese captured Earhart and she became Emperor Michinomiaya Hirohito's sex slave.

Perhaps it would be propitious not to solve the Earhart mystery. Let it linger for those who follow. A beguiling mystery stimulates mental acuity and communication.

FIN

PHOTOGRAPHIC GALLERY

Amelia Earhart

Vice Admiral
Marc Mitscher

USS Franklin, CV13

George P. Putnam

Edward C. Elliott

Lockheed Electra Model 10A

A-E's Lockheed Electra Model 10E Special

Frederick "Fred" Noonan

Howland Island

USCGC Itasca

Chief Petty Officer Radioman Leo Bellart, USN

Commander Walter K.
Thompson, USCG

USS Colorado BB 45

Vought O3U Corsair

USS Lexington, CV2

Paul Mantz

President Franklin D.
Roosevelt

SMS Sharnhorst

IJN Shikshima

League of Nations Flag

Japanese Flag

Lieutenant Col Earl (Pete)
Ellis, USMC

Howard Hughes

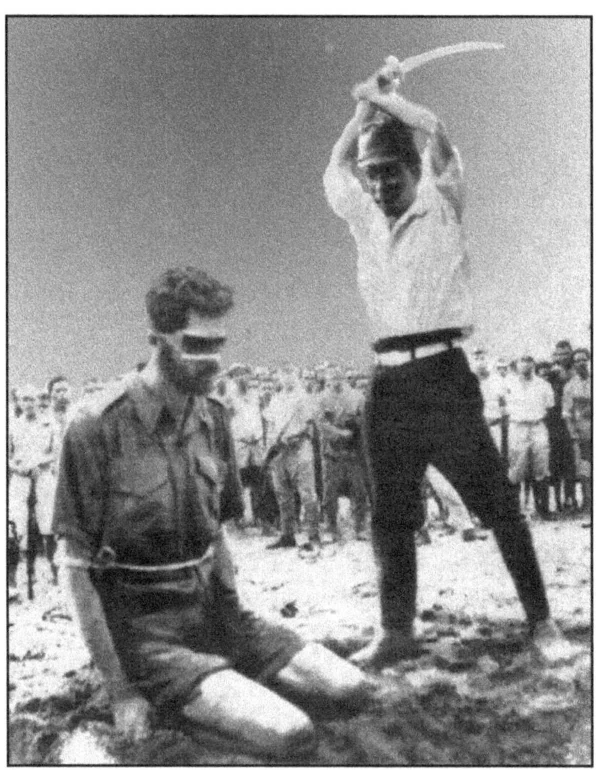

Keneitai Execute Ellis

Commander Joseph
Rochford USN

Admiral William H.
Standley, USN

Captain Haynes Ellis, USN

Japanese Kwangtung Army
Seizes Manchuria

Admiral Earnest J.
King, USN

Rear Admiral
Earnest J. Kirk,
USN, CNO

Fairchild-Camera KA-17

Consolidated BPY Catalina

Beechcraft SNB

Eastern Airline DC3

Pan American Airlines Logo

Pan American World Airways Clipper Ship

Boeing Model 314, Flying Boat

HDQS. Bldg. Naval Air Station, Alameda

Hughes Tool Co. Logo

Hughes Tool Co. Abandoned Hangar

James Roosevelt

SPINTCOM

CINCPACFLT HDQS Makalapa, Pearl Harbor

Honolulu State Library

Vertical Aerial Photograph

Mrs. Eleanor Roosevelt

Eugene (Gene) Vidal

Cordell Hull

Nazi Germany's National
Socialists Swastika

USSR Comintern Emblem

Condor Legion

Benito Mussolini

Japanese Army Enters Changchun, Manchuria

Henry H. Woodring

Juan Trippe

Claude A. Swanson

Kempeitai

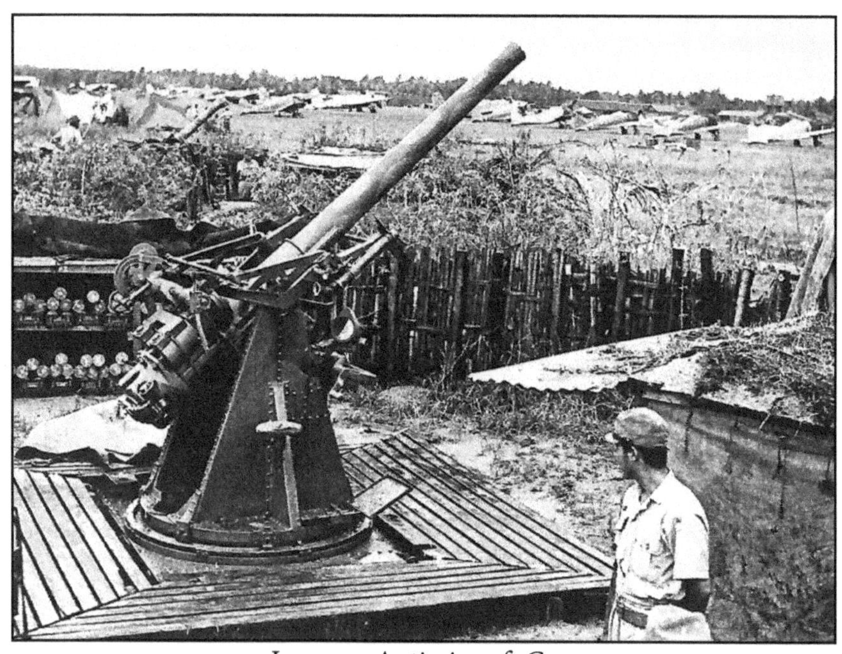

Japanese Anti-aircraft Gun

Mitsubishi KI-15

Amelia Earhart

Air Traffic Controller with Aldis Lamp

Electra Departs Lae

Nauru Airfield

USS Franklin Afire

ERIKA

The low-cut gown fits the lissome Erika Dubois as if it were a thin coat of white paint—revealing far more than it ought. Set well apart, her green eyes flash with wicked sin, and her velvety red hair is a celestial fire at eventide. Dripping with rented, glimmering jewelry, she saunters into the casino. At forty-four, Erika is the most beautiful and seductive woman in the room—notwithstanding the several dozen gorgeous young starlets dressed in clinging gowns and clutching their cinema moguls. All eyes turn to Erika as she waits in the foyer to be escorted to a table. She forces an acid smile, acknowledging the patrons' recognition.

Erika is broke, and her career has faded. For too many years, the sensuous Erika was the premier sex persona in Hollywood. Her pictures were lavish and risqué, and a couple were *avänt-garde.* Her sensuality oozed off the screen. Though, only a moderately competent actress, her pictures earned enormous profits for the studio. Unfortunately, four money-sucking husbands, a lavish lifestyle, four divorces, and the stock market crash in 1929 left her destitute.

The Hays Motion Picture Production Code of 1930 installed a moral censorship system that forced the studios to produce family-oriented films— overt sexuality was proscribed. The Hays Code sealed her fate. Conforming to the Code, her studio produced two more pictures staring Erika. In the first, she was a school marm on the Western frontier. In the next, she played a young widow with two children. Both pictures were duds. Her arrogance, unreasonable demands, refusal to accept the changing mode of the picture business, and the budget cuts engendered by the Great Depression doomed her career. The studio cancelled her contract, citing violations of the morals clause.

Her pride would not allow her to work for the minor studios in "B" pictures. She was the "star" and would always remain so. She tried to form her own production company but could not garner financing—money was too tight, her reputation was soiled, and ticket sales were weak. Her friends did not return telephone calls, and executives would not schedule an appointment. In effect, she was blackballed.

Tonight, perhaps, is her last chance to resurrect her career. Erika knows that Cáspár Gazda, *l'enfant terrible* producer of several of her earlier pictures and her last two flops, is attending the Cannes International Film Festival. He's looking to cast the female lead in his new epic film, *Cleopatra.* She desperately needs the Cleopatra part.

The *maitre d'hotel,* in his white-tie evening dress, glides over to welcome Erika. "Good evening, Miss Dubois. Welcome to the Grand Hotel casino. How may I be of service?" he asks with smarmy affection. "A table?"

"Yes." She scans the room with the eyes of a huntress. "Who is that young man sitting alone by the double windows?"

"His name I do not know. He is an American on some business here and is a guest in this hotel."

"A table close by."

The host escorts Erika to a table next to the windows and seats her so that she faces the American. She orders Chandon's Dom Pérignon 1922, and looks over the room with a cat-like eye to locate her former producer. She spots Cáspár Gazda and mutters inwardly, *That Hungarian bastard is at the roulette wheel with that hussy, Madeleine what's-her-name.*

The waiter fills Erika's flute and she resolves, *I'll inveigle him later. Meantime, I'll beguile that handsome American.* She knows well that her image demands that she have a handsome male companion for the evening. With a slow smile, she stares shamelessly at him. Catching his pale-blue eyes, she raises her glass in a toast, and then empties her flute. The waiter promptly refills it.

Unaccustomed to such blatant flirting, the American's cheeks flush red with embarrassment and perplexity. Nonetheless, he smiles weakly, raises his glass in a return toast, and bows his head slightly in acknowledgement. He is tall, six feet plus, and his black hair is cut short, his chin is square, and he sits erect and confident.

Erika summons the waiter. "Ask the fellow at that table in front to join me." She taps his arm and asks, "What's that he's drinking?"

"Whiskey, Madam. Bourbon whiskey."

"Egad! A primitive."

Soon, the American is standing next to Erika's table. "Good evening, madam." He bows slightly. "Thank you for your invitation. I am pleased to join you."

"Sit, young fellow." She smiles seductively. "First, I'm not a madam. I do not manage a bordello—however, the idea has some merit in these strange times." She laughs at her little joke. "Now, I'm a Mistress—divorced too many times from too many self-centered, lay about husbands. The bums!"

The waiter sets a flute in front of the American and fills it with the champagne. "Thank you, Miss Dubois. I recognize you from your pictures."

"That's swell. Always willing to entertain a fan. Drink that wine and tell me about yourself, and what you're doing here." She looks at him and winks. "Drink up. Don't be bashful. I don't bite. Well, not usually."

Ill at ease, Todd looks down and speaks in his soft Texas drawl. "I am Theodore Wilkerson from Midland, Texas. But everyone calls me Todd." He glances at her and forces a small smile. "I graduated last May from Texas Tech University in Lubbock." He sips the wine and continues, "I majored in petroleum engineering, and in the summers I worked in the oil fields as a roustabout. That's Dad's mantra, 'Start at the bottom'"

Feigning curiosity, she asks, "Tell me more, Todd."

"The Penwell field is just south of Odessa—the largest in West Texas. It's our family's. I'm learning to take over the business and let Dad retire." He looks up, smiles, and empties his flute.

Oblivious to the import of his comments, Erika comments with a touch of condescension, "That's wonderful for you, Todd." She raises her flute to sip but it is empty. She hails the waiter. "Another bottle, and keep 'em coming."

Todd continues. "I've always had a keen interest in motion pictures, so Dad sponsored this trip to the Cannes Festival as my graduation present. When I return, I'll work on a rig as a drill hand."

The orchestra begins a Strauss waltz. Erika rises and says, "It's a waltz. Let's dance." They are a striking couple as he leads her gracefully about the floor. For the moment, she forgets her mission and enjoys fully her companion's deft skills and his gentle attention. Next, the orchestra plays a fox trot. Todd leads her expertly; she closes the gap between them and rests her head on his shoulder. Next is a lively Charleston that they conquer with brassy aplomb. The room is abuzz at the pair's exhibition. Following is a tango, and Erika plays the part of the seductress to full measure. As the music ends, Todd is awkwardly embarrassed as he returns the actress to their table. "Please excuse me, Mistress Dubois."

"Of course, dear lad."

Todd heads for the men's room.

Erika cracks a slow smile and purrs to herself, *I still got IT.*

With his composure restored, Todd returns. "Never have I had a dance partner as skillful as you, Mistress Erika. That dance set was wonderful. Most of the girls at school can dance the 'Cotton-Eyed-Joe,' the two-step, and 'Put Your Little Foot'—that's about all."

Erika smiles broadly and says, "You amaze me, Todd. You're a superb dancer. Where did you learn?"

"My mother and older sister taught me."

Impressed with this shy, well-mannered, and obviously family-oriented fellow, she demands, "Give me your fountain pen."

He reaches into an inner coat pocket and hands it to her.

She scribbles on the napkin. She leaves her chair. "Stand up, Todd." She puts her arms around him, kisses him full on his lips, and says, "I'm delighted to have made your acquaintance. You're a gentleman of the old school. Not many of your type in Hollywood. You're one of the few men I've met that didn't try to get into my knickers on our first date. Perhaps too many have." She slips the napkin into his coat pocket. "That's my telephone number. If you ever get to Los Angeles, call me, and we'll do the town. I leave you now, my new friend. I've business that I must attend to. Toodle-oo." She walks quickly away.

Todd, slightly tipsy, elated at meeting Erika, the famous motion-picture star, and confused by her abrupt departure, returns to his table, and orders a bourbon whiskey, straight.

Erika moves to the roulette wheel and stands next to Cáspár Gazda. "Good evening, Cáspár. It's nice to see you again."

He looks up, places a five-hundred franc chip on number thirteen, and says, "Hello, Erika. You look lovely. You and that young man on the dance floor raised a considerable stir among my friends. Who is he?"

She pooh-poohs the question. "A nobody. Not our type. Give me a few minutes of your time. Let's talk at the bar."

With a resolute voice, Cáspár Gazda responds, "Erika, I'm with Madeleine De La Rue, and I don't have anything to say to you. We concluded our business several years ago—with some acrimony, as I recall."

To Gazda's right is the young actress, Madeleine. She is a stunning, bleached blonde: tall and well-proportioned. She's not wearing a brassiere and her haughty breasts struggle to escape from the confines of her blouse.

Erika gently puts her right hand on Gazda's shoulder and looks him in the eyes. "I've made a ton of money for you and the studio. Let's talk."

He brusquely removes her hand and says, "Good night, Erika."

With a bit of menace in her voice, she whispers, "All these years, Cáspár, I've kept our secret rendezvous at your cabin at Big Bear Lake confidential. Let's talk at the bar."

Realizing that Erika has played her blackmail card, Gazda tells Madeleine, "I'll be gone only for a few minutes, stay here." He rises, looks at his stack of chips, glances at his date, and puts the chips in his pocket. He walks to the bar.

Erika orders champagne cocktails and tells the *garçon de comptoir,* "Put it on Mr. Gazda's bill and add a generous gratuity." With determination Erika demands, "I want the part of Cleopatra. You know I can play that part to perfection."

Gazda looks across the room, thinking of his response. "Erika, Cleopatra is twenty-one years old in my picture—her age when she seduces Caesar. There is no way you can play this part with conviction and engender audience empathy."

Not to be deterred, she pleads, "With proper make-up and hair style, I can do it. I know it will work and we'll have a great picture—just like ol' times."

With some sympathy for the aging and desperate former queen of the cinema, he says, "No, Erika. I've cast Madeleine to play Cleopatra. The deal is signed and sealed." He empties his glass and turns to return to the roulette table. "By the by, my wife during our halcyon years at Big Bear Lake died three years ago."

The crowd of reporters, photographers, and newsreel cameramen surround Erika as she stands on the steps of the Grand Hotel. Flashbulbs pop incessantly. She is dressed in an elegant Victorian gown, her hair is tied in a bun at the back of her head, and bifocal glasses cover her green eyes. She raises her hand to quiet the news people. "Please, only one question at a time."

Hildegard Lancaster, the maven of the cinema press, emerges from the group. Her outrageous hat is cocked at a rakish angle. With pen and notebook in hand she says, "Congratulations, Erika. You've never been better, and your film *Catherine* will become an all-time classic. Brava!" She scribbles a few notes and continues over the whirr of the Mitchell and Wall motion-picture cameras, "Please tell us what motivated you to play Catherine the Great when she was fifty-six years old? Your acting made her character come alive and leap from the silver screen into our hearts. After "The End" faded to dark, the standing ovation was the most enduring and intense I've ever witnessed."

Erika smiles broadly and makes eye contact with the crowd. "Thank you, Hildegard. For the first time in my career, I had total artistic control of my picture: I wrote, produced, and directed *Catherine*." She opens a large leather bag hanging from her left shoulder, withdraws the award, and waves the *Grand Prix du Festival Internationale du Film* over her head, and shouts, "Thank you, Hollywood. I've found my own way."

Hildegard says, "Congratulations on your artistic triumph. But, Erika, you've been away from the studio system for years. How did you find financing for this independent epic in these hard times?"

"It's supposed to be a secret, but what the Hell. My picture's executive producer, a marvelous angel, is an old pal from West Texas—an oil man."

MY MORNING KISS

Dixie leaped onto my bed, dug out the covers hiding me, flopped next to me, and gave me a big, sloppy kiss full on my mouth. Sleepy-eyed, I nonetheless grabbed my favorite pal and kissed her back. She wagged her tail feverishly. Dixie is a loveable, stubborn cuss of a three-year-old Labrador. Her inbred job is to rule this household. On awaking, she assumes the task of the reveille bugler—everybody get up. I'm sure she was trained by a tough Marine drill sergeant in her previous life. Though unsaid, her orders are, *"Rise and shine. I'm up. I need to go outside, and where's my breakfast? Roll out of those sacks and let's get this day moving."*

Dixie

I looked out the window and saw frost on the glass and snow on the grass and trees. My room was warm and snug. I asked myself, *Isn't it Saturday?* I stroked Dixie's head several times and said in a firm voice, "Dixie, there's no school today. Besides, it's too cold to get up. I ought to be able to sleep in." I climbed back under the covers.

Dixie would not be deterred. She whacked me on my shoulder a couple of times with her front paw.

"Son," shouted Mom. "Breakfast is ready."

Dixie kissed me again and pulled the covers off the bed. *"You dummy, it's Friday."*

Reluctantly, I crawled out of bed and put on my long pants—my first pair, at nine years of age; buttoned on a long-sleeve, red shirt; slipped on my wool socks; and laced up my Buster Brown oxfords, newly bought from Joske's Department Store. Dixie supervised my activities with watchful eyes—ready to whack me should I skip a step or fail to carry out the routine precisely.

The aroma of frying bacon and percolating coffee permeated our small home. Mom, always up early and dressed in freshly-pressed clothes, conducted her morning scrutiny to ensure that my clothes were spick-and-span, homework completed, and books packed, and that I was ready for the mile-long walk down the aspen-lined gravel road to the Hicksville school. I knew that when I returned, Dixie would be waiting for me at the gate with her tail wagging lickety-split and ready with a big, sloppy kiss.

Dixie led me into the kitchen; I slipped in the breakfast nook, and began eating. Dixie knew that she was not allowed in the breakfast nook, but she sat at the opening, patiently waiting for treats she was not supposed to have. Secretly, I broke Mom's rule.

My name is Charles, and I'm home on leave from my second tour in Afghanistan. This morning I went to that copse of aspen trees where Dixie and I used to hide. I straightened the cross over her grave and wondered who she is kissing nowadays.

SALLY

Sally is the meanest horse I've ever met. She hates me. And, I hate her. Well, I really don't hate Sally. I'm just leery of her. Last summer she bit me on my right arm. It required seventeen stitches in the Emergency Room, a tetanus shot, and antibiotics. My arm was in a sling for a couple of weeks. Being right-handed, I had a miserable time coping. Nonetheless, in about a month I decided that perhaps Sally and I could come to an understanding and we could ride again. I love to ride, especially Sally. When we're riding she seems to metamorphose into another personality. She's happy and docile. She prances and swings her tail wildly; she's queen of the trail.

Anyway, as I approached Sally she whinnied loudly, bared her teeth, and dared me to approach. I bribed her with two carrots and a handful of sugar cubes. With minimal protest, she let me saddle her. Off we went. It was a bright, sunny, autumn day. Some of the trees had begun to turn to gold. We took the long trail along the Pedernales. At the falls, we entered the crystal-clear water. Sally drank, and then back-kicked her front leg to splash the cool water on her underside and me. We rode down the river on its smooth, rocky bottom. Sally was having a fine time. So was I. After a couple of miles, we entered the trail home. As soon as we stepped onto the trail, Sally spotted a diamondback sunning itself. It was the biggest diamondback I'd ever seen. Sally bucked and reared, throwing me. I fell nearly on top of that serpent.

In a flash, the diamondback coiled and struck. Not me, but Sally. Sally, seeing the danger, wheeled to stomp on that reptile. The diamondback hit Sally full in her chest—injecting that deadly poison near her heart.

I blew the head off that damned rattlesnake with a round from my Colt 45. Sally was down—foam oozing from her mouth. She looked at me with those big brown eyes. I stroked her nose, but in a few minutes Sally expired. I loved that wonderfully brave horse with all my soul.

BERNIE AND ME

We heard her screams from our hiding place across the street. By "we," I'm referring to Bernie and me. Bernie was my longtime pal and a likeable cuss. A month older than I, he was smart, honest, and mischievous—always conjuring up impish vexation and conning me into being his aide-de-camp.

It wasn't what we did, but rather the aftermath that wrecked our summer vacation.

Ol' Chief McAfee, head of our Tonopah police department, was first on the scene. Soon, it seemed, the entire gendarmerie of our town, all three of them, were on the scene—taking photographs, measuring distances, mapping trajectories, and interviewing witnesses. With horses running hard and snorting, and bells clanging, our town's lone fire-wagon arrived. The volunteer firemen pulled out the hoses, attached nozzles, and pointed them. With no smoke visible, they could not figure out where the fire was. In a jiffy, the white-clad, emergency fellows tumbled out of the ambulance wagon, pulled out the gurney, and stopped dead. "Where's the victim?" we could almost hear them shout. Without leadership and direction, these folks rushed about in chaotic patterns. The scene looked like organized pandemonium.

Bernie and I viewed the unfolding panorama below from a dense grove of quaking aspens atop the hill on the west side of the village square. It was late afternoon, so we were backlit, which made it nearly impossible for those in the square to see us. If we had been attuned to the future, we'd have decamped. But no, it was too much fun. We couldn't hold back our giggles and guffaws. The scene was so delicious that we were helpless with mirth—we couldn't stand. We rolled on the ground making a rumbling ruckus.

Here's the deal, if you must know. Early that morning we had borrowed that stuffed gorilla in Bernie's Uncle Amos' attic. He supposedly had shot that ape on an expedition to central Africa in '98, shortly after he charged up San Juan Hill with Teddy and the boys. We all knew that his ape story was malarkey. He bought that gorilla in an antique shop in Eureka. But to keep in his good graces—his treats were sumptuous—we pretended to believe his wild tale.

Anyway, back to the story. While my maiden Aunt Esmeralda was attending church, we hid the gorilla in her closet, dressed it in her white lace gown, and crowned it with her white chapeau—the one with the red ribbon, placed at a rakish angle on the ape's head. Then we buckled her black high-top shoes on its feet. To complete the ensemble, we stuck one of my dad's 5¢ cigars in the gorilla's mouth.

As you might suspect, we were quickly unmasked. In our merriment, that ol' biddy Mrs. Cornelia Rathskiller spotted us. Now, let me tell you about Mrs. Rathskiller. She was a widow and had more money than she could count. Inherited it from her late husband, "Big Buck"—don't know his real name. Two years ago, he got knifed in a crooked poker game in Silverbow. He owned that gold mine up the road in the Toiyabe Range. She was the town gossip and busybody. Since she owned most of our town, we kowtowed to her. Anyway, knowing Bernie and me and our penchant for monkeyshines, she reckoned we were the culprits. We spotted her scurrying over to Chief McAfee. Well, I reckon you can figure out the rest of the story—but not quite, I'll bet ya.

In the reckoning, Bernie's dad sent him to St. John's Military Academy in Elko for the rest of the summer and the next two school terms. My dad restricted me to our home and press-ganged me into a ten-hour day, six days a week—slave labor in his hardware store for the rest of the summer.

By the time we graduated from high school, our isolationist Congress, at President Wilson's urging, had declared war on Germany and Austria, and the good ol' U. S. of A. was in the Great War—the War to End All Wars.

President Woodrow Wilson, 1914

Bernie joined the Army. Immediately after basic training, he was sent to France with the American Expeditionary Force. In the battle of Chateau Thierry, Bernie single-handedly charged through no man's land to knock out a Hun machine-gun nest. He didn't make it. He lies in the American military cemetery at Epinal, France.

I joined the Navy. Figured I'd have three squares a day and a dry bunk each night. I was assigned to the "four-stacker" destroyer *USS Wickles*, DD-75. I worked in the deck gang, and soon was promoted to boatswain-mate striker. En route to Queensland, Ireland, only a dozen or so miles off the coast, our squadron ran into a German wolf pack. Our skipper focused on the closest submarine. We depth-charged that sub and sank it. For the rest of the war we were on patrol in the North Sea. We didn't see any more action.

Tonopah, Nevada, 22 August 1941

Bernie came home last evening, planted a big kiss on my cheek, and hugged me tight. Bernie, he's my number-one son. Bernie's the Chief Boatswain Mate on the battleship *USS Arizona*: home-ported in Pearl Harbor.

USS Arizona, BB39

GENERAL WU

Kansu Province. China,

Spring 1919

General Wu drove his saber cleanly through the terrified monk's throat. Wu snatched the heavy jade statuette from the monk's hand before the fellow fell. The statuette was an icon from the Tang Dynasty, 200 BC—worth a small fortune on the black market in ancient Chinese artifacts.

General Wu

Wu is a hefty man—easily 70 kilos, and over two meters tall. He exudes an imperious mien—head straight, shoulders back, long, confident strides. His large, daring black eyes command fear and awe. Mounted on his Takli Mongolian horse, he bellows orders to his ragtag army of mercenaries, "Mount up and follow me."

Wu is the warlord of Kansu Province. He rules with unmitigated cruelty. Yet strikingly, he is a learned and cultured man: earned a bachelor's degree in mechanical engineering from Peking University, writes poetry, sings Chinese opera, and plays the violin with deft skills.

You may wonder what General Wu has to do with me—a demobilized digger. A few months after the Armistice, I was a civilian again and chose to stay in China to make a fair dinkum fortune. I was knocking about in Tsingtao looking for an assignment, without much success. As diggers are wont to do, I drifted into the Lost Lamb pub on Ling-po Road and ordered a Foster's in my newly acquired Mandarin. After a pint or two, I began flirting with a "lady of the evening"—a beautiful White Russian, a woman of a certain age down on her luck. Not reaching an agreement, I kissed the sheila on her cheek and said, "Toodle-oo."

I turned and started chatting with a Japanese officer in his native tongue. This bloke was a member of the occupying contingent in charge of a construction battalion repairing the damaged dockyard. We tossed a few pints while discussing how quickly the Japanese marines had routed the Germans in this treaty port.

As I was about to leave, another fellow introduced himself—said he was Lieutenant Chin Lo-sey in General Wu's irregular army in Kansu Province.

I acknowledged him with a hearty, "G'day, mate. How may I be of service?"

It followed that we smoked a couple of pipes—his treat, of course. He was impressed with my language skills—Mandarin, Japanese, a smattering of Russian, and of course English—not the King's English, mind you, but the "down under" English of a jackaroo from the outback in Queensland. He said he would recommend me to serve as General Wu's interpreter, if I were interested. The monthly salary he offered was exorbitant—more money than

I've made in my lifetime. And the pay would be in British Pounds Sterling, mind you, not in Chinese funny money.

In a few days, I received a telegram from Wu. Hired me on the spot. He needed my language skills because patrols from the Japanese Kwantung Army had made sorties into Kansu Province to test his strength. And, General Chang Kai-shek was preparing a campaign to root out the warlords in China's northwestern provinces.

Additional duties were to teach English to his brood of fourteen children and to his extended family—three wives and I don't know how many concubines.

Wu is an enigma. In his residence compound, most often he is a loving puppy: caring, tender, and devoted to his number-one wife, Huwang Mae-ling. I might even say he is obsequious from time to time. Please understand, it is Mae-ling—the Qizi—who rules the residence. Wu caters to his children with loving affection. Spoils them all. Treats his servants with respect. He is a model father, husband, and lord of the manor, as it were.

Yet he can be commanding and brutal when crossed. For instance, a few weeks ago he flogged the concubine Lee Chi-shi, whom he suspected of having had a tryst with a gardener. Too bad, she was a classic oriental beauty. He had the gardener impaled on a spike on the compound wall.

Sometimes he is just plain scary. When annoyed, I've seen him draw his saber and slash at whatever is nearby: person, animal, thing, or structure. Last week, he sobbed bitterly when, in a murderous rage, he killed his favorite horse.

Today, I'm on the dole again. Wu is with his astral ancestors. A couple of days ago he commanded the sufficiently recovered Chi-shi to come to his bed. She did. Later, as he snored next to her, she plunged a dirk into his heart—such as it were.

I RECKON

Grandma Mattie died last week. Sad. But, not so sad, actually. I hardly knew Grandma Mattie. Only visited her a couple of times before mama left. Matilda was her real name, but ever since I can remember, everyone called her "Mattie." Don't even know how old she was. Pretty old, I reckon. Don't know why grandma expired. Probably it was meanness and old age.

She lived by herself on a scrubby plot near Vanderpol. About four-miles east. Grandma Mattie was cantankerous to her core. And tight-fisted too. I reckon she had a right to be. Grandpa died in a train wreck near Lulling in Caldwell County some years ago. He was the engineer. Soaring Texas heat popped the spikes and the rails spread. His train flipped over and… The funeral was grand. Mama and I went. Lots of neighbors, piles of food, fancy fiddling, and lots of visiting in this out-of-the-way place. Most folks seem to have a fine time. Grandma Mattie didn't seem so happy. About the last time I saw her.

Anyway, Sheriff Willard, in Bandera County, sent me a letter to tell me the sad news. Had the County seal, some Latin words, and other official folderol. He wanted me to come down there to make arrangements. I don't make arrangements. Don't have the wherewithal or inclination. And I don't have an automobile or a horse, and the Greyhound bus doesn't go that way. Besides, next week I'm working in Mister Egan's hardware store. Hunting season starts in a couple of weeks. I sent a letter to Sheriff Willard asking him to bury grandma Mattie in a potter's grave.

I want you to understand. My home is on a little spread about a mile out of town, my parent's place. I farm a little on a couple of hardscrabble acres, vegetables mostly. Do odd jobs for folks in town. Hunt for my meat. Lots of game in the hill, wild turkey and deer mostly. Sometimes I land a big-mouth bass in the lake. But that's almost leisure time.

Hoot'n and Holler'n Honky Tonk

Some years ago papa vamoosed with that floozy barmaid at the honky-tonk. Her dresses were so tight that her boobs popped. And she worked it to a fare-thee-well. What she saw in papa I'll never know. He wasn't pretty. Drank too much. Had severe body odor. Always was flat broke. And he had a vile temper. reckon mama and me were better off without him.

Mama and I got along OK. She worked at the five-and dime six days a week. I worked odd jobs here and there. After a bit, mama got sick. A peculiar sort of sickness. She would wander about, miss work, not speak. She didn't make sense most of the time. I tried to take care of her, but she got worse. One day last July two medical orderlies from our hospital came to our house in an ambulance and took mama away to a sanitarium, a bedlam for all I know. It's in Langtry over in Val Verde County. Once in a while I would visit mama. Waste of time. She didn't know me. She did nothing except sit and stare, spittle dripping from her mouth. I reckon that makes me an orphan.

The county tax collector confiscated Grandma Mattie's house, the land, and all the furniture and stuff inside to pay back property taxes. Left was an old trunk in the attic. Sheriff Willard says not much of anything in it. Nothing of value anyway—a pair of high-top shoes, several granny dresses. I reckon they were made from flour sacks, two bonnets, unmentionables, a mother-of-pearl comb, bundle of letters from mama, and an old family Bible. Didn't want any of grandma's stuff. Told Sheriff Willard to give it to charity.

I reckon that's what he did mostly. Anyway, last Tuesday I got the Bible. Sheriff Willard packed it up and mailed it. One of these days I'll send him a Railway Express check for his expense. I don't read the Bible much. Last night, while lying in bed, I pop it open to scan the front pages. The Genealogy pages go five or six generations. Never heard of most of these folks. Like most families, I reckon some were righteous and some were blackguards. Don't know, and don't much care.

None-the-less, this morning my curiosity about this Bible got the better of me. I started fanning the pages, looking at the pictures. And sure enough it popped open on the New Testament page where Jesus tell the Pharisees, "… render therefore to Cesar the things that are Cesar's." Staring me in the face was a spanking-new $10,000 bill. Not just an ordinary $10,000 bill mind you, but a gold certificate. Numbers emblazoned in gold ink. The reverse entirely in gold. Grasping for breath, I nearly fainted.

Two steaming hot coffees later, propped on my foot stool, my senses recouped: what was I to do with this bounty? I never imagined so much money. I need new boots. Get a horse? How about a tractor? Move to Abilene in Taylor County? Nah. I like it here. How about fixing the roof? Too many decisions. What a quandary.

Later that afternoon, I went to the Post Office. Dropped that gold certificate in a stamped-envelope and sent it to the Salvation Army. They would use it better than I would. I reckon.

MADELINE

Madeline slaps Randolph with all the power she can muster. He reels backward slamming into the bar knocking over glasses and bottles. She screams, "You cheating bastard. How could you?"

Randolph wipes the blood from his mouth as he rises from the floor. "What the Hell are you doing? Have you gone mad?"

"No, but you have. You slept with my best friend." With a more reasoned voice, she laments, "Proxy boasted about her seduction of you to her roommate, and Charlene leaked it to me."

Proxy, seeing the ruckus, saunters to the bar, puts her arms around Randolph, and kisses him with her mouth full open. Breaking the embrace, she contemptuously spouts, "Randolph is mine now. Go back to your mangy hound. He'll love you. Maybe."

Madeline, with tears streaming down her cheeks, lifts her skirt, draws her Walter PPK from the holster on the inside of her left thigh and empties the magazine into Randolph and Proxy. Calmly she remarks, "Fornicate on your way to Hell!"

THE KIT

My pal Jesse survived that cat attack—but, just barely. Mind you, this cat was not an ordinary household pussycat but a 220-pound cougar—panther, puma, mountain lion—powerful, cunning, and aggressive. With a full-speed bound, that cat hit Jesse solidly—knocking him catawampus off the trail and into the gulch, some 20 feet below. His camera and tripod sailed into the forest.

Gingerly, I approached with my Colt 45 drawn. The cougar, its mouth blood-stained, stared at me—challenging me to come closer. I froze. Get Jesse was the goal, not kill the cougar. I fired three rounds into the air. The cougar was not fazed by my shots; it continued to stare even more intently, I imagined. If it charged, the next shots were for the cougar. For an eternity, it seemed, we stared at each other in the classic "Mexican standoff." In a minute or so, the cougar bounded into the forest. And, that's the way it happened.

Here's the background: Last October we were near the summit of the Toiyabe Range in Nye County, photographing Ophir, one of the most well-preserved ghost towns in Nevada. As we are wont, we were on our annual ghost-town photographic tour. Great fun. Lots of fabulous ruins to photograph. The sky was crystal clear—at this altitude it's almost purple. Leaves were gold, scarlet, and topaz. Stringy altocumulus clouds broke up the solid purple and told us that snow was approaching.

Jesse was hurt seriously—gashes on his head and neck, and flesh hanging from his shoulder. Blood everywhere. I wrapped his wounds with gauze from our First Aid kit, as best I could. With lots of effort I got him into our truck and started the drive down the mountain—a 50-minute, bouncing, four-wheel drive, and across two fast-running creeks. Jesse was awake. Not saying much. Obviously in serious pain.

A couple of hours later we got to Austin via Highway 50 (the loneliest highway in America, boast Nevadans). Damn! This burg had three casinos, two service stations, and three bordellos, but no doctor, no medical center, and no EMS folks. Speed limit be damned. In another hour, Jesse was in the Emergency Room at the Fallon Hospital. Fifty stitches later, and with a tetanus shot, antibiotic shot, and a hearty dose of morphine, Jessie was dreaming of better days, in his hospital room.

I talked with the sheriff and the game warden. They wanted to go after that cat and capture or kill it. I argued, no. The puma was defending its territory, the natural thing to do. We were the trespassers. We should have been more watchful.

After three days, Jesse and I were headed home. He would need several weeks of rest and months of therapy. Scared something awful. But he would be OK.

I didn't want to waste a day of this gorgeous autumn. Accordingly, a weeks later I was ghost-towning again. With me was Rick—a long-time pal from my USC Cinema days. We were photographing the ruins at Hamilton in White Pine County. An outstanding ghost town, with dozens of structures scattered over a square mile or so. In the late 1880s, Hamilton was the second largest town in Nevada—second only to Reno. Hamilton died quickly after the silver lode played out in the early 1900s.

Opera House, Hamilton, Nevada

I was setting up to photograph the one remaining brick wall of the Opera House. Rick was about a half-mile down the trail photographing the fallen-down Masonic Hall.

Hamilton, NV, Withington Hotel, White Pine County

I was framing the scene when it occurred to me that I was hearing a faint, doleful cry. Spotting nothing this side of the wall, I walked around.

Immediately I spotted the source. A puma kit was trapped in the rubble—a timber across its front leg. Probably had been chasing a rabbit or an opossum. In its zeal it must have hit a cross timber, knocking it loose. Now, I may be dumb but I'm not stupid. I left that scene as fast as possible. Climbed into our truck and shut the windows. Mama puma must be close by and en route post haste to rescue her kit. I recalled all too clearly what had happened to Jesse last week. I wanted no part of the upcoming scenario. That mama puma really is going to be in a tizzy trying to free her kit. And, she'll be irascible at me for messing around.

Five minutes later, no mama puma. Ten minutes later— same. Twenty minutes later—ditto. Only two possibilities: She is hurt or she is having a tryst across the mountain. Eventually, my compassion and curiosity overwhelmed my good sense. With some serious trepidation, I pulled the timber off the kit as it yelped repeatedly. It could not move—leg broken. Using my

Boy Scout training, I fashioned a splint out of wood splinters and tied it off with strips of my handkerchief. None too soon, I might add.

Bounding down the mountain at full speed was mama. No doubt, she had spotted me handling her kit. Retreating to the truck, I watched mama pick up the kit by the nape of its neck. She walked to the truck, put her front legs at the base of the window and stared at me. I have to tell you her slitted, green eyes were terrifying. Might as well be a lioness in the savanna in Kenya. Deadly. Soon, she trotted toward the mountains with her kit. As you might suspect, I'd left my camera by the wall and I didn't get a photograph of any part of this scenario. *C'est la vie.*

Nonetheless, I continued to explore and photograph the ruins. In a small box canyon across the creek, I spotted a nearly complete wood cabin. Perhaps an opportunity to photo some paraphernalia left inside—chair, table, boots, who knows. I peeked inside. Dark as Hades. Scanned the floor inside with my flashlight before entering, on guard for rattlesnakes—a favorite place for them to linger. None spotted. Faint light filtered in from two partially boarded windows. To the rear was a dresser with the middle drawer open, tattered coveralls hanging out. I set my camera on the tripod, framed the shot, set the flash, and fired. The light bounced off the walls, illuminating the interior for an instant. Maybe a fine shot.

The earsplitting roar was terrifying. Spinning around, I spotted mama puma and her kit just inside the front door. I was in her den. Trapped! No other way out. I froze—in deep trouble. She stared at me with those steel-green eyes, taking my mettle. Ever so slowly, I moved my right arm to my left shoulder to draw my Colt 45. I didn't make it. She advanced with a deliberate pace. Her eyes focused on me. Something in her mouth. If I were to move any more—well, I reckon you know the outcome. My right arm hung suspended in midair, sweat trickling into my eyes, time stood still; she moved closer.

A couple of feet away, she stopped, looked into my eyes, and dropped a dead rabbit at my feet. What the? Licked her whiskers. I might have prayed. Don't recall. Nearly fainted though. Amazingly, she started rubbing her back against my legs. Back and forth. Back and forth. Back and forth. Don't recall how long. A minute or two, for sure. Is she warming her dinner? Did manage to get my right arm relaxed by my side. Then, more amazingly, she started nuzzling my hand with her nose.

Mama Cougar and her Kit

It took me several seconds to recover and understand. With great care, I slowly knelt. With my fingers extended, I started scratching her head and back—ever so gingerly. She purred—much as a household pussycat would. Her kit, with the splint, approached. Watched intensely. Still super-frightened, I continued to scratch. Adrenaline surging. Question above all others: How do I escape this scenario with all my fingers and my overall well-being? She answered. Licked my face, grabbed her kit, and bounded out of the cabin.

Rick didn't believe me. My friends didn't either. Wife thought I was liquored up. And, I reckon you don't either. Never mind. Next time I'm at Hamilton, I'm going to get that puma to sign an affidavit.

RAQUEL

A *roman à clef*

Sailors tell sea stories—a tale of some incident in the sailor's adventures that is memorable, at least to the sailor. By definition, sailors enhances their tales with fictional events to make it more compelling for his shipmates. The following tale is without the sea story enhancement. It's as faithful to the facts as best as I can remember.

In February 1968, I reported aboard the aircraft carrier *USS Ranger (CVA 61)* as ship's company. I was a Special Duty Officer, Air Intelligence. We deployed to the Tokin Gulf in October 1968 and conducted air interdiction operations primarily in North Vietnam. My primary task was to develop targets for our Air Group to strike.

The ship's routine was to conduct air operations for seven consecutive days, stand down for one day, and then resume flight operations for the next seven days. Because of the nature of my job, planning targets for the next day's operations, I had to work on the stand-down day to insure that the next day's targeting was ready for briefing the aviators, ordnance officers to plan appropriate weapons for the targets, and ordnance men to load such weapons on the aircraft.

Most of our intelligence shop was in the air-conditioned spaces—necessary to keep our banks of computers from overheating. Unfortunately, the targeting shop was outside the air conditioning boundary. It was in a small vault on the deck just below the flight deck and beside the Admiral's ladder.

Inside we had maps of the Top-Secret Vietnam air war posted throughout the vault. We had a small fan to circulate the air, and when we were inside, we keep the vault door open to help circulation. We rigged a drape over the vault's door, and posted a large "KEEP OUT" sign in the center of the drape. No unauthorized sailor ever entered my vault.

As luck would have it, the Bob Hope's Christmas USO Tour flew aboard late on 21 December 1968 shortly after we'd completed air operations for the day. Included in his troupe were Les Brown, his Band of Renown cinematography crew and staff, and the starlet of the year, Miss. Raquel Welch—one gorgeous and sexy dame.

Raquel Welsh, *USS Ranger*, Christmas, 1967

Next day was our stand down day and that afternoon Bob Hope put on one terrific show. God love him. I know he and Bing are playing sub-par on that golf course in the celestial sphere. Of course, Raquel was a terrific hit. After the show, I returned to my vault to complete the targeting plan for tomorrow's strikes. I closed the drape over the door and became fully immersed in my targeting tasks. Time slid by.

A soft, throaty female voice snapped me back to reality, "Can you tell me how to get to the enlisted dining hall? I'm supposed to have dinner with Seaman John Jones."

I whirled around and saw Raquel standing a few feet from me. Startled, I was momentarily without voice. She was inside my Top-Secret vault—an incredible breach of security. Nonetheless, she was wearing a form-fitting blue micro-mini skirt, three-inch high heels, and a skin-tight, brown knit blouse over a no-bra, *brassière*. The visual effect was erotically stunning and mind numbing.

Still without voice, and shocked that my air war might possibly be compromised, I rose from my chair, placed my right hand on her left shoulder and turned her around so that she faced the drape. With a gentle nudge, I guided her outside my vault. No words were exchanged.

Fortunately, a sailor was walking down the passageway. I said to him, "Seaman, take Miss. Welch to the enlisted mess." A large smile cracked on his face and without ado, they scrambled down the Admiral's ladder. That's the end of my sea story. But it's no sea story. My tale is about as accurate as I can remember some forty-five years later.

I've wondered, from time-to-time, if I should have slammed the vault door shut with Raquel and me inside. Dream on.

STERLING CITY

It was a classic Western blizzard—one of those intense winter storms that assault the mountains without warning, seeming to come from no-where. We, that is, Chuck and I, were trapped at the 9,500-foot level in the Independence Mountains in northern Nevada. The north wind was howling, and the driving snow was so thick that visibility was just a few feet. The temperature was dropping precipitously.

Please understand, we're not stupid. Perhaps we're a bit off-kilter but certainly not stupid. Safety is our primary consideration—having a fun adventure is secondary. We've been ghost-towning in Nevada for a dozen years or so, and we have a keen understanding of how capricious the weather can be in these parts. Usually, we plan our trips for mid-autumn, when the weather is "just right"—not too hot and not too cold. The creeks and washes no longer run with summer snowmelt; they run gently. The deep-blue sky is clear, and the sun is low on the horizon. The acute-angle sunlight engenders fine shadow detail in our photographs.

Let's review. Before shoving off that November morning, we had checked the Weather Channel. The forecaster predicted that the early winter storm brewing in the Canadian Rockies would hit northern Nevada two days hence. That morning the clear sky was almost purple. To the north were smatterings of high cirrus clouds—the precursor to that approaching storm, days away. All in all, it was a positive manifest for a "go."

Our goal was to find and photograph the ghost town dubbed Sterling City and Mining Camp, which had been abandoned around 1890. This site is seldom visited because of its near inaccessibility—it's almost at the summit of the mountain. We four-wheeled ever so carefully up a steep, twisting, and precipitous mountain trail that our topographic maps showed as the route.

We did not get far up that seldom-traveled trail before we encountered sections littered with rocks of all sizes and broken tree limbs. It was a time-consuming task to clear the trail so we could proceed. As we climbed higher, we encountered numerous washouts that we had to fill with rocks, brush, and mucky soil. About halfway up, we encountered small patches of snow left over from the last storm—no serious impediment. After four grueling hours of some of the most difficult travel we'd encountered in all our ghost-towning adventures, we spotted a tall brick chimney towering over the quaking aspens. Inching forward, we broke into a small valley and were awed to see a reasonably well-preserved mining camp—an outstanding reward for our tough journey. In a preliminary exploration, we were pleased to find that vandals had not ransacked Sterling or sprayed it with graffiti.

Coke Ovens, Sterling City

In the background, atop a small hill, were five coke ovens in moderately good condition. At the south end of the valley were four large leaching ponds, each holding a deep layer of liquid green "goop." The sign posted at the entrance of this complex read, "DANGER, CYANIDE." Below the lettering was an image of a skull and crossbones. We took a long shot of the area, including the sign, and then skedaddled back to the main site.

Dominating Sterling City was a gigantic A-frame over an open mine-shaft. The area was littered with expensive mining equipment—diesel motors, huge flywheels, ore crushers—and all manner of detritus. Outside the mining-operation complex were several wood and brick buildings, some with roofs caved in, and others almost intact. Inside several of these structures, we found hundreds of core samples in small white bags, each carefully annotated and stored in an arrangement we could not decipher. Also inside were scales, instruments of all sorts, office furniture, and file cabinets, some of which had folders and "stuff" jammed into them. Indeed, because of its extensive and reasonably well-preserved structures, and its near-pristine condition, Sterling Mining Camp is one of Nevada's premier ghost towns. What caused the owners to abandon Sterling and leave all this expensive equipment behind? We surmised that the mine played out and the owners decided that it would cost more to move this stuff down the mountain than it was worth. Or the company went bankrupt and did not have the funds to salvage what was left of their mining operation.

After several hours, we completed our photography. Satisfied with our good fortune at finding such an exceptionally well-preserved site, we continued four-wheeling up the mountain to photograph the workers' housing complex about a quarter mile away. En route, the sky had quickly clouded over. When the first snowflakes hit our windshield we were startled, and our inner alarms blared "get out of this place *tout de suite*." Too late. In a matter of minutes, the fast-moving winter storm hit with tempestuous fury. Clearly, an extended four-wheel drive down that treacherous mountain trail, now covered with snow and perhaps ice, was untenable.

Because visibility was almost zero, I trudged up the hill in front of the truck to guide Chuck through the blinding snow. Soon, I was covered with that white stuff and nearly frozen.

Nonetheless, we made it into the housing complex and stopped at the first structure that had a complete roof and door. Inside the one-room cabin were a steel bed with springs, dresser, two chairs, a cracked mirror, and other paraphernalia. Being old hands at ghost-towning, we always carry survival gear for summer and winter. We unloaded enough equipment to last for several days: sleeping bags, blankets, warm clothing, food, portable stove, water canisters, a high-powered rifle—mountain lions and other critters also would be seeking shelter—and other supplies. And of course, books. Chuck prefers action/adventure novels which feature exotic *femmes fatales.* I tend toward the Raymond-Chandler-type detective story that features a hard-boiled dame in a low-cut gown with a gat in one hand and a flagon of champagne in the other.

Shelter, Sterling City

We settled into our "palatial" home, and tried to use our cell phones to communicate with the sheriff's office in Elko County to tell them we were stranded in Sterling City but doing okay. Before we left Elko that morning, we had stopped at the sheriff's office to let them know our plans and say we'd check back with them after we returned. Not surprisingly, our cell phones were useless in this remote place.

Before we fired our portable stove, Chuck ambled over to the one window in this palace to open it a crack to ventilate the harmful gases emanating from the stove. Then it happened. The wood floor beneath him gave way and he fell about two feet to the ground. He uttered a small cry as his right foot slipped and turned on an obstruction.

I helped Chuck climb out of that wooden trap. His ankle was turned, nothing more serious. We figured it was a rock that his foot had hit and forgot about it. Later, with time on our hands and boredom overwhelming us, I suggested that we remove that rock and cover the hole with wood planks from one of the other huts so that we'd not repeat that incident. The cover would also block the cold draft blowing into our cabin.

Well, glory be! That obstruction was not a rock. It was two leather sacks stamped with the mark of the Carson City Mint and jammed full of gold coins. We dumped the coins on the floor to see what they were and to take inventory. I've never believed in the tooth fairy, but that day I wasn't so sure.

We counted one thousand $20 "double eagle" coins dated 1893, uncirculated—fresh from the mint. We were looking at a small fortune in gold. But that would be a pittance compared to its real value. As a youngster, I had dabbled at coin collecting and have some basic knowledge of this hobby. This cache's true worth lay in its numismatic value—a fabulous amount beyond my ability to estimate.

The questions were: Who had secreted this treasure here? Why? When? After some speculation, we reckoned the bags were stolen. The desperadoes must have skedaddled out of here for parts far away—before the Law found them. Their best tactic had been to hide the gold coins, with a plan to return and recover their treasure when the notoriety of their robbery calmed. They didn't want to be captured with that booty in their saddlebags. On reflection, such musings were not completely satisfactory. They did not answer the questions about who and when. There had to be more to this narrative. And, there was.

In our zeal to retrieve those two bags, we hadn't further explored the ground. I got to the window, tipped over the wood planking covering the hole, and used my flashlight to see if anything else was stashed below. There was. A well-worn leather satchel lay a couple of feet to one side. I retrieved it. Inside was another treasure trove.

Butch Cassidy

First out was a copy of the Winnemucca Gazette dated July 31, 1899. The headline blared in 20-point type, "Butch Cassidy Gang Robs Union Pacific Train." The lead article reported the details of this daring robbery. To summarize, it said that on the previous day Robert Lee Parker, known as Butch Cassidy, and another bandit, speculated to be his close ally Harry "Kid Curry" Logan, both members of the Wild Bunch Gang, had held up the number 501 Union Pacific train as it lugged itself up Soldier's Pass in the Osgood Mountains, just a few miles east of Winnemucca. Stolen from the baggage car were two bags containing an untold number of $20 gold coins. The Carson City Mint was sending this gold to banks in the small towns along Nevada's main east-west railroad, which parallels the Humboldt River.

The two masked bandits had burst into the baggage car with six-shooters drawn. Logan had quickly disarmed the two Pinkerton guards and forced them to lie on the floor. Meantime, Cassidy shoved his gun in the back of the attendant's head and forced him to open the safe. He did. Logan and Cassidy snatched the two bags and the pair leaped off the slow-moving train as it inched its way up the steep pass. That was the last seen of these two brigands.

The article reported that Pinkerton Detectives were marshalling forces to find and arrest the highwaymen and to recover the loot. Sheriff Jim Langtry confirmed from passengers on the train that Cassidy and Logan had been riding in the passenger car behind the baggage car. As the train slowed, on some signal from Cassidy, the pair had walked quickly to the front of the coach and exited. The passengers' descriptions fit known resemblances to Cassidy and Logan. And that was about the end of the newspaper story.

Also in that satchel were several letters to Robert Parker from his sister, Esmeralda, in Salt Lake City; a paid receipt for four dollars from the Silver Dollar Hotel in Virginia City for two nights lodging; and two Union Pacific passenger ticket stubs—$34 dollars paid for two one-way trips from Reno to Salt Lake City.

Mystery solved. We were fabulously wealthy. We were euphoric—in "hog heaven," and we speculated for hours about how we would spend this fortune. We realized that we had to be careful how we sold these coins so as not to arouse questions. We'd liquidate a few at a time to numismatic dealers around the country, and from time to time we'd offer a few on internet auction websites.

The next day the storm passed. Sunshine bathed the valley and the temperature rose. A mild west wind washed the mountain. The snowmelt made the trail down the mountain impassable—it would be a mass of slick mud, so we had to wait a few days for the trail to dry.

After two days of fantasy, reality set in. This treasure trove did not belong to us. It was not "finders keepers." These gold coins belonged to the Federales. If we kept them, we'd be outlaws—accessories to the Wild Bunch Gang's robbery. And if caught, we'd spend years in a federal penitentiary.

The only prudent and honorable action was to return these coins to the federal attorney in Carson City. Well, that's exactly what we did. Got a handshake, congratulations, and a detailed receipt.

Several months later, I received a form letter from the Attorney General: "Thanks for your honesty…" and all that government blather. An intern on his staff would check to see if a reward had been offered for the return of those coins. The ensuing federal silence was deafening. About a year later, an envelope arrived from the Treasury Department. In it was a check for one thousand dollars—a pittance compared to the millions those coins were worth. Included in the envelope was government Form 1099, which showed that I owed $324.76 income tax on the reward. C'est la vie.

On the whole, I'm not a vengeful person. However, the Federales' reaction to our integrity was beyond the pale. Not in anger or hurt, but in disappointment, I ripped the check into several pieces, marked Form 1099 "NOT VALID," put the remains in an envelope, and returned them to the Treasury. And that's the end of my yarn.

Well, not quite. What I've left out was, there were actually 1,001 coins in those two bags. Probably a clerk at the mint got distracted and miscounted. We kept that odd-man-out "doubloon." Flipped for it. I called tails and won.

On the appointment of my thirty-five-year-old daughter as federal attorney for the Eastern District of California, I gave her that coin as a memento of my brush with the legend of Butch Cassidy and the Wild Bunch Gang.

WHITE SHORT SHORTS

I was minding my own business, sitting at a table sipping my latte at the Coffee Now on the second floor of the indoor Acme Forever shopping mall. I turned my chair so I could view the passing scene down that long isle with the specialty shops on its left side. This is a gambit of mine that I use to foster ideas that could germinate into a short story or perhaps even a novella.

For a time, nothing noteworthy passed by or happened. Then, while I had the coffee cup to my lips, a flash of white passed close by me. It came from my blind side so I did not see the whole scene. A second later, I damn near dropped my cup. It was a young woman in white, very short-shorts that were tailored to fit skin-tight and enhanced every curve of her derriere. A glimpse of her cheeks peaked out from the seams of those white, short shorts.

Her legs were willowy, golden-tanned, and delightfully shaped. She walked with a steady, purposeful tread down the aisle in erotic syncopation—a walking advertisement for her profession, I reckon. I couldn't see her face as she strolled away from me down the aisle. Yet I wondered if her face were only slightly soiled.

For reasons I cannot explain she whirled about, walked briskly toward me with her eyes blazing and searching for mine. Before I could rise to greet her, she slapped me square in the face with a force that knocked me to the floor, my glasses flying, and my latte catawampus. She spouted with venomous hate, "You dirty ol' fart. Lecher after someone else."

THE BAY OF PIGS

Author's Note:

Images of certain persons and objects mentioned in the text are posted in the Photographic Gallery at the end of the text. The images are in number order.

The letter's return address was International Sales, Inc., with a Post Office Box in Abilene, Texas. I'd never heard of this outfit—even though I'm from Fort Worth, not that I know everything about Texas. I'd returned to my room after I'd completed my mid-watch in the ship's Intelligence Center— ready for a long, and well-deserved sleep—"sack time" in Naval parlance. Working 12 to 15 hours every day these past two weeks on various targeting options, I was the target analyst on the World War II aircraft carrier USS Essex, CV9. Found the letter on my bunk. Unusual. 'Cause most of our mail is distributed at our work stations. Probably just more junk mail. Not interested. Tossed it on my desk.

I collapsed into my bunk—dead tired, body and mind, after my shower. Clicked on my overhead light to read for a few minutes—helps clear my mind. Picked up on my left-off place on Dashiell Hammett's The Maltese Falcon. The gentle rolling of the ship began to relax me. After a few minutes of reading Caspar Gutman's, (the "fat man") famous quip, "…but we were talking then. This is actual money, genuine coin of the realm, sir. With a dollar of this you can buy more than with ten dollars of talk," something began stewing in the back of my mind. The "something" gradually came into clear focus. That letter. The stamp was the four-cent commemorative stamp honoring Simon Bolivar. That's peculiar. Junk mail doesn't have a first-class stamp nor a return address.

Rolled out of my bunk and slit open the letter.

Dear Lt. Sanderson:

We understand that in a few weeks you will be released to inactive duty and will continue in the Naval Reserve as a Special Duty Intelligence Officer and that you graduated first in your class at the Armed Forces Air Intelligence School at Lowry Air Force Base in Denver. Congratulations. (How the Hell did this outfit know that?)

We deal in international trade and are interested in talking with you about long-term employment. Upon return to Fort Worth, please give us a telephone call. Our representative will contact you for a preliminary interview.

To cut to the chase, as it were; International Sales is a proprietary company for the Central Intelligence Agency—the "outfit," the "company", the "agency"—the CIA. (1) In the intelligence business, a proprietary company is a wholly owned subsidiary of the CIA. Such an enterprise engages in a for-profit business. On the black side, well you can guess.

Three interviews later, one almost all-day with several agency types, a two-day physical exam, completion of a 24-page application (wanting to know my genealogy for the past hundred years, it seemed, and everything about my past life), and information needed to grant me the required Special Compartment Intelligence clearances; I got the call to come to Langley, Virginia for processing. (2) I was hired.

My first assignment with "The Company" was to the Directorate of Science and Technology (DS&T). After a few weeks of orientation, I was detailed to the National Photographic Interpretation Center—the "NPIC"—located in the Navy Yard in Washington, DC. (3) After a six-week intensive training program, I was ready to tackle my first assignment—photographs of the Soviet's Baikonur Cosmodrome launch site in central Asia—Kazakhstan, to be specific. (4) As I developed professionally, I found the work challenging, demanding, and wholly satisfying.

At NPIC we examined all manner of photographic imagery—aerial, motion picture, ground-based still photographs, and photographs from our satellites in the CORONA and SAMOS programs. (5) With state-of-the-art instruments, we saw images in stereo—giving us the ability to measure depth and to get a detailed perspective of the objects in the photographs. Additionally, we supplemented our black and white photography with infrared and radar imagery.

Significantly, when we compared photographs of the same area that were taken on different days, we garnered important intelligence; oftentimes it's the change in activities that offer the best clues as to what's happening and why it's happening. All-source intelligence, signals intelligence (SIGINT) for example, (6) we produced imagery interpretation reports for The Company, the Executive, the Defense Intelligence Agency, (7) and other intelligence agencies of our country. From time-to-time we shared reports with our military allies.

But, I digress. Ever since Fidel Castro (8) overthrew President Fulgencio Batista on 23 February 1959, rumors swirled that we, the US of A, would do something about it—not tolerate a communist Cuba at our back door. Of course "something" was not defined, but we guessed it was an invasion. As the Eisenhower presidency wound down in 1959, the scuttlebutt became more intense.

After John Kennedy took office in 1961, (9) the invasion crystallized into a definitive Operation Plan—dubbed "Puma." President Kennedy tasked The Company as the lead agency to plan and execute "Puma". The Company would train and arm some 1,500 Cuban expatriates to form a military brigade for an invasion of Cuba—Brigade 2506. (10) The Company's 20 Douglas B26 attack bombers provided air support. The B-26s were based in secret bases in Nicaragua, and at Dill Air Force Base in Florida. Pilots and crew were former members of Batista's air force and CIA contract members of the Alabama Air National Guard. The Navy was scheduled to use Douglas A4

(12) and AD (13) attack aircraft, operating from carriers USS Essex (14) and USS Shangrila. All Navy aircraft markings to be obliterated—pirate aircraft, no less.

Our first task was to get high-definition photographs of Cuba with emphasis on beaches, lines of communication, military installations, air fields, radar, and anti-aircraft artillery (AAA) emplacements. (15) Within days, our U-2 high-altitude reconnaissance aircraft were criss-crossing Cuba with their high-resolution image systems capturing, on film and other sensors, every geographic, military, and economic characteristic of the island. Of particular importance was the Cuban order-of-battle—military equipment availability, where, and condition. At the tactical level, (16) Navy F8U-2P photoreconnaissance aircraft took low-level aerial photographs of tactical targets that NPIC designated and incorporated into the Bombing Encyclopedia, as well as the target list in Puma Operation's Order.

The U2 aircraft is an amazing product of creative thinking and engineering—half airplane and half glider with altitude capability in excess of 70K feet. Cruising speed about 500 mph. (17) Its nickname is "Dragon Lady," after the exotic female-pirate in the comic strip "Terry and the Pirates" of the mid-1930s. Built by Lockheed Aircraft of Burbank, at their "Skunk Works" under the supervision of Chief design engineer, Clarence "Kelly" Johnson. (18) Flight testing was done at the Groom Lake Test Site (Area 51) in Nye County, Nevada. (19) Its first flight was on the first of August 1955.

At the time, the U2s flying at 70,000 feet were out of the range of Soviet interceptor aircraft and Soviet surface-to-air missiles (SAMs). (20) The primary Soviet SAM was the SA-2, NATO name "Guideline." Soviet radars tracked the U2 flights but were impotent to intercept. However, in May 1960, Gary Powers was piloting a U2 over the Soviet Union when he had engine trouble and lost altitude. A Guideline, surface-to-air missile shot down Power's U2. You know the rest of the story.

The sensor suite on the U2 consisted of an array of high-definition cameras arranged for horizon-to-horizon coverage, panoramic coverage, and other sensor "stuff." To complement the sensor suite a contract was let to Eastman Kodak Company to develop an extremely high resolution black-and-white film with an acutance that would resolve with great clarity a razor-thin straight line. This new high-resolution was dubbed "T-grain." This film in the U2's camera suite had a resolution of 12 inches at 70,000 feet.

Immediately, we had trouble—lots of trouble. The film from the U2s and the F8U-2Ps was processed at the Fleet Air Photographic Laboratory (FAPL) at the Naval Air Station (NAS) Jacksonville. All too frequently, the processed negatives were unacceptable—too opaque or too light, laced with dirt particles; wrinkled, ripped, and stretched. We could not discern the tactical targeting and strategic information we needed for the Agency to properly plan the invasion scenario. No matter our communication with the Photographic Laboratory at Jacksonville, film processing did not improve. Time was pressing and we had no solution in sight.

The next morning I contacted Capt. Norman Leman, USN, the Commanding Officer of the Naval Photographic Center, (21) and laid out our problem. He knew exactly what to do. Within the hour, the Personnel Officer had prepared Temporary Additional Duty (TAD) orders for Lt. Michael (Red) Ryan, Photographic Officer on-board the USS Essex, to report to the Fleet Air Photographic Laboratory at Naval Air Station, Jacksonville. His task: do whatever is necessary to get those aerial-film processing machines "fixed."

Lt. Ryan had the reputation, well deserved, that he knew more about naval photography than any sailor in the fleet. Ryan was a mustang—rising through the photographer's mate rates to Chief Petty Officer—the highest enlisted rate, then commissioned Ensign as a Limited Duty Officer (LDO), Photography. "Red" was a stocky fellow with flaming red hair; a rebel with a salty tongue and singular dedication to the photographic task at hand.

At the Naval Air Station, Anacostia, DC, a Beech SNB utility aircraft with its right engine ticking over was standing by. Ryan and I boarded. (22) Take off was smooth. No matter my attempts to engage Ryan in conversation, he remained stoically silent. Three hours later we landed at NAS Jacksonville. A waiting sedan took us to the photographic laboratory.

"Red", energized, charged the lab's front door. Yanked it open. He tore off his service dress blue jacket, festooned with more medal and campaign ribbons than I've ever seen on one sailor. Ripped off his tie. Tossed both on the Duty Officer's desk and bellowed, "Where's are those fucking aerial processing machines?"

Red worked 48 hours straight. We kept him functioning with a sandwich now and then and gallons of hot coffee, some spiked with medicinal brandy—courtesy of the duty Chief Corpsman. With the help of photographer mates at the lab, "Red" first dumped all the chemicals; ran a diluted acid solution through the processing machines; disassembled the machines; cleaned and polished every roller, tine, rod, and the interior wall to a spotless sheen; mixed new chemistry to precise specifications; checked their pH (a measure of their acidity and they were on specifications to two decimal points); filled the tanks with filtered chemistry and wash water; set the temperatures precisely; and ran a test strip. Results: perfect. He ran three rolls of yesterday's U2 film through the processing machine and the film was clean and beautiful. Shadow areas showed extraordinary detail. Highlights were not blocked. I scanned several of the 12" by 9" frames over a light box and was absolutely amazed at the clarity and resolution of the images. Problem solved.

"Red" got his tie and jacket, stomped out of the lab, and demanded to know where was the fucking Officer's Club, "It's happy hour. If not, I'll make it so."

A couple of months later, in a private ceremony at Central Intelligence Agency Headquarters, Director John McCone (23) awarded the Agency's Distinguished Intelligence Medal to Lt. Michael Ryan, USN. "Red" stood at perfect attention in his Dress Blues, festooned with his array of awards. As Director John McCone read the Citation I detected an ever so slight smile on "Red"—first ever, I suspect. Next day at the Naval Photographic, Captain Leman pinned the Navy's Meritorious Service Medal on Lt. Ryan. Don't know how he remained erect with all that metal on his chest. Last I heard of "Red" he was attached to the Marines 5th Regiment as a combat photographer in Viet Nam.

At NPIC we viewed thousands of feet of superb aerial photography. Using all-source intelligence, we decided that the optimum landing site was near the town of Trinidad on the south-central coast of the island. Within a few days Navy frogmen clandestinely took beach samples. The Trinidad site had many of the desirable properties required for a successful landing and the push inland, for example, a wide solid beach with hard sand and no obstructions. A few hundred yards behind the beach there was an excellent road that ran parallel to the beach, and there were several roads that branched off this parallel road that led to the interior and to major highways. There was a fine seaport, and additionally, the rugged mountains a few miles southeast of the city afforded an operations area where the members of Brigade 2506 could fall back and establish a guerilla campaign were the landing to falter. The clincher was that several Cuban expatriates convinced us that the population of Trinidad was generally opposed to Castro—not true, in hindsight. Invasion date was set for 17 April 1961.

In mid-March, the CIA changed plans and recommended that the invasion site be the Bay of Pigs instead of Trinidad. Reason: Nearby was a first-class airfield for the B26s, and other considerations. President John Kennedy agreed. What a slam! We had not focused our intelligence activities in this area. Now, we had only a few weeks to prepare a new Operations Order; and to garner, evaluate, and disseminate tactical intelligence. We did not complete the task.

Starting on 15 April, the Company's B26s attacked Cuban airfields, including Antonio Maceo International Airport at Havana. Such attacks continued for the next three-days. Unfortunately, most of the B26s were shot down by Castro's Air Force and anti-aircraft fire (AAA). The remaining few, most with serious damage and wounded airmen landed at Key West or ditched in the ocean. President Kennedy, at the last second, issued orders for the Navy to stand down: do not launch aircraft. Without air superiority, the invasion had little chance to succeed. Actually the invasion was doomed. Castro's intelligence organization, Revolutionary Armed Forces Intelligence, knew exactly where and when the invasion was scheduled. Such was the case because of a Brigade member's loose talk in Miami, and at Dill—Castro's agents in the Brigade. And perhaps more importantly, the Soviet's KBG (24) had all the details which they relayed to Castro.

Starting at midnight on 17 April, Brigade 2506 went ashore at the Bay of Pigs and other beaches nearby. I reckon you know the rest. Castro's armed forces defeated the Brigade in three days. About 110 Brigade members were killed and 1,200 captured. (For a myriad of reasons, a few did not make it to the beach.)

I stayed in the Directorate of Science and Technology for the next thirty years, retired to my family ranch near Fort Worth, raised cattle, grew roses, and taught a course in intelligence at Texas Christian University (TCU). (25) End of story.

Technical Data

Sensors on the U2 are:

- Total of 2.5 tons of reconnaissance equipment.
- Perkin Elmer Corporation developed the optical camera system. The Hycon model A-2 camera system, consisting of three K-38 framing cameras rigged in a trimetrogon arrangement: two 24-inch (lens focal length), f8.0, side-looking cameras (right and left) with 9.5" wide film; and one 24-inch vertical camera.
- 9.5" is the actual width of the film. The image area is 9 inches square.
- The trimetrogon camera arrangement provided continuous horizon-to-horizon coverage.
- Resolution of the vertical camera system is about 12" at 70,000 feet.
- Length of a roll of 9.5 inch film is 2,000 feet, and weighs 270 pounds.
- One K-38, 3" panoramic camera with 2" wide film
- Other sensor "stuff."

T-grain Film

The process of producing film is to sensitize an acetate base by extruding silver-halide crystals onto this base. In this process the crystals group into a myriad of various sizes and odd configurations. Accordingly, such film does not have a uniform layer or arrangement of the crystals. For ordinary photography the sharp resolution and fine granularity of such film was satisfactory—served us well for many years. However, its resolution, granularity, and other sensitometric properties do not meet the precision needed from the photographs taken at U2 altitudes and speed.

In a brilliant breakthrough, Kodak engineers and chemists developed a process that forced the individual silver-halide cubic crystals, suspended in a layer of gelatin, to form in a three-dimensional trapezoidal "T." Fitting together like identical pieces of a jig-saw puzzle, the dense assembly of these tabular grains produce a near uniform film emulsion. Some wags contend that on the film exposed in the U2's cameras we could read the printing on a golf ball. I'm not convinced. It was sharp, but not quite that sharp.

PHOTOGRAPHIC GALLERY

1. CIA emblem

2. CIA Headquarters Building

3. National Photographic
Interpertation Center

4. Baikonur Cosmodrome

5. Samos Reconnaisance Satellite

6. SPINTCOM

7. Defense Intelligence
Agency

8. Primer Fidel Castro

9. President John Kennedy

10. Brigade 2506 soldier

11. Douglas B-26, Invader

12. Douglas A4 Skywarior

13. Douglas AD-1 Skyraider

14. USS Essex CV-9

15. Lockheed U2 Reconnaissance Aircraft,
Dragon Lady

16. Chance Vought F8U 2P Photo Rconn

17. Dragon Lady

18. Clarence L. Kelly Johnson

19. Groom Lake, Area 51, Test Range

20. Soviet SA-2 Guideline 2

21. Naval Photographic
Center, Anacostia,
Washington, DC

23. John McCone,
Director CIA, 1961

22. Beechcraft SNB

24. KGB

25. TCU

THE BUZZ

heard that familiar and terrifying buzz before I saw the coiled and ready-to-strike diamondback about a foot from my left leg. Its camouflaged design and coloring blended closely to the sagebrush background. I froze. I was stuck. To move in any direction would cause that venomous serpent to strike.

Western Diamondback

I was hiking on a narrow winding trail in the Davis Mountains north of Alpine, Texas looking for a spot to photograph the upcoming sunset. A few moments ago, I'd frightened a jack rabbit that scooted into the underbrush.

With beads of sweat dripping off my head and neck, and my heart racing, I tried to devise an injury-free escape plan. Unexpectedly, I heard this high squeaky voice, "You dumb jackass. You spooked that jack that I was counting on for dinner. Just how dunderheaded are you? I ought to get the ASPCA on your butt."

"What the…? I looked about and saw no one. "Who's speaking?" I shouted.

"Look down here by your foot, you nincompoop. It's me, Ms. Diamondback, that's trying to get your attention, and who is about to send you to the hospital—if you make it."

What's happening? I swirled around again and saw nobody. "Madam, whoever you are, please show yourself." This does not make sense. Rattlesnakes do not talk.

"It's me OK. In addition, I'm not speaking. I am sending you messages *en clair* via the diamondback telepathy network. Now, get with it."

This is just not happening. I must have entered a wormhole and am in a parallel universe.

"Taint so, birdbrain. You're right here on terra firma and, man, I'm getting pissed. I've waited three days for dinner and I'm hungry. Listen up, dumbass, last spring I had a tryst with that handsome fellow up the trail, and I've got nine young ones on the way. How am I gonna feed them without that jack?"

Resolved to the absurdity in this scenario, I said cautiously, "Ms. Diamondback, my sincere apologies for spooking your dinner. Here's a deal. I'll find a jack rabbit. Shoot it. And bring it back to you. How's that for a plan?"

"That's no damn good, addlebrain. I'll not swallow your buckshot and get lead poisoning. I gotta kill it to eat it."

"Well, what do you suggest, Ms. Diamondback? Got any ideas?"

"Yeah." She raised her head a bit. "I'm gonna strike you 'cause I don't like your looks, and the world's got too many ignoramuses as you are anyway. Stand by while I figure where I'm gonna hit on your cadaverous body."

Carefully, I'd been moving my right hand to the holster on my hip. While she was fuming, swinging her deadly head back and forth, and increasing the buzzing to peak pitch, I drew my Smith and Wesson 38 special and blew the head off that smart-ass serpent. I don't cotton to diamondbacks in any way and especially not to those that mess up my afternoon. Smugly proud of myself for evading yet another crisis, I failed to notice that the nine little diamondbacks in her womb had spilled on the desert floor.

I heard that voice again, this time in echoes, "We know what you did. We know who you are. And we're gonna get you!

DAGMAR

If my supervisor says, "No" to my request for a raise in salary then I'm standing up and walking out the door. He'll wonder if I'm leaving this company and accepting that job offer from Acme Fertilizer, Ltd., or am I meekly returning to my cubicle and pressing onward as before and finishing the details on the Paramount Mountain account. Actually, I'll do neither. I'm going to the railroad station and catching the Western Flyer to Miami. I'll lie around on the beach, sip exotic cocktails, lecher after the bikini-clad babes strolling by, and patiently wait for his telephone call. He knows that only I know about the $250,000 kickback he got under the table from that outfit in Abu Dhabi. I have a copy of the contract in my safety-deposit box.

A couple of days later, at sundown I was sipping a rum-based cocktail dubbed "Hurricane" on the hotel's patio, watching the passing scene. Before I was aware, she stood before me and asked, "May I sit at your table? All the others seem to be occupied."

"

Dagmar

Startled at the lovely vision before me, I stood and stumbled, "Yes. Of course. Please share my table." I pulled out the vacant chair, smiled my best, and indicated for her to be seated.

She glided into the chair, flashing her long and shapely leg, and gave me that large "thank you" smile. "I'm Dagmar Seville from Reno. The next round will be my pleasure. What are you drinking? I prefer the Manhattan with Wild Turkey bourbon."

Not yet fully recovered, I stumbled. "A Hurricane, please." I've seen lots of beautiful women in my days, but Dagmar was near the top in feminine pulchritude. She was tall and willowy, with golden-tanned skin and a mane of sun-streaked auburn hair. Her mouth was large and sensitively carved with a dangerous smile. She had a curvy figure in a clinging white dress, slit high and tailored to fit very tight. She flashed her wide and crystal-clear green eyes, and she toyed with a gold chain hanging between her generous breasts.

I responded "I'm Cody McCollum from Fort Worth."

"How nice to meet you, Cody." She leaned forward, exposing more of her bra-less bosom than she ought, "Just Dagmar, please."

The waiter brought our drinks and she suggested we toast to our new friendship. "Cody, do you know that fellow at the bar? He keeps staring at me."

I turned around, spotted the fellow, and concluded I did not know him. "Don't know him. He's probably having a vicarious experience by lech-ering after you"

"Perhaps." She replied.

We clicked glasses and I took a long and deep swig of the Hurricane.

I vaguely remember the flashing red lights and the screaming horn and a couple of fellows doing things to me. I do not know how long it was but the next I remember was the fellow standing in the fog next to my bed. "Mister McCollum, I'm Doctor Gil Miller and this man is Detective Sergeant Joseph Foxworthy from homicide. Can you hear me clearly?"

Befuddled, I nodded my head positively.

"You've been poisoned with a substance we've not yet determined. Until we get a toxicology report, we can't administer an antidote. Unfortunately, your vital signs are deteriorating rapidly and, to be perfectly honest, I doubt that we can save you. Do you understand me?"

"Yes."

"Who should we notify?

"Dagmar."

"Who is Dagmar? asked Sergeant Foxworthy.

"The Hurricane."

Foxworthy said, "Next to your bed is a court reporter. Do you understand that you are dying?"

"It can't be."

THE CONDOR LEGION

Basque Country, Spain

26 April 1937

Oberleutnant Hans Schaeffer leans over the optical instrument and speaks clearly into the intercom microphone that is just an inch from his lips. "Right three degrees." The twin-engine Heinkel model-111E eases ever so slightly to the right. Three seconds later Schaeffer speaks, "Right one degree." The roar of the engines is deafening. "Steady." He pauses. "Steady." "Steady." He pushes the thumb button on a long cable. "Bombs away." The Heinkel jumps a little.

Heinkle He 111

Schaeffer looks out the large Plexiglas windows of the bomber's nose and sees the string of fifteen SC 250 bombs hurling downward to the un-armed town below. In another second, he sees dozens of other bomb strings from the other twenty-three German bombers on this morning's raid.

Schaeffer cracks a slow grin, speaks into the microphone, "Pilot Hauptmann Dietrich, on target. Look below."

Dietrich glances out the side window, sees the hundreds of bombs bursting inside the town, and shouts "Good morning Guernica. The Condor Legion sends you our wakeup call."

CHARLIE

harlie's limp was pronounced. The clack, click, clack, click of his steel cane on the cobblestone street held me in stupefying suspense. The street was so dark that I could only see a moving outline coming toward me. That woman told me to stay here, remain still, and let Charlie approach. I was mesmerized. The closer he came to me the more intense was my disquiet. Damn, I was gripped with apprehension.

The last time I saw Charlie he looked to be sixty-years old though I knew he was only forty-two. It was that ragged, red scar on his face that ran from his chin to his forehead, his premature gray hair, and his perpetual grimace that belied his age. He was tall, lanky, and slightly stooped. However, what I remember most were his jet-black, widely spaced eyes that spoke of evil incarnate.

The racket stopped. Charlie was standing right in front of me. Without provocation, he thrust his right hand directly toward me. Reflexively, I grabbed that hand and cried, "Hi dad."

BOAZ

In 1935, shortly after the Italians conquest of Abyssinia, I led a team of archeologist from the University of Turin, and we discovered a clay tablet in a small cave in the Entoto Mountain Range. The symbols were in ancient Hebrew. Serge Belli, the team's linguist translated the text.

It read:

I am Boaz, the third son of King Solomon and the first son of the Queen of Sheba. I am my father's scribe and scholar. Shortly after my mother died, my father charged his Egyptian physician to perform the mummification process on her body. There was a brief ceremony to mark the end of her life. Afterwards my father tasked me to return the queen to her birthplace in the highlands of Africa. Befitting a queen of Israel, servants dressed her in a fine gown. Retainers lined her casket with gold, spices, and precious gems. They placed her casket on a cedar-built cart pulled by four oxen Her cortège consisted of 50 soldiers, 50 mourners, and 50 slaves. We traveled across a raging sea, and across a sunbaked desert. We waded in an endless muck that was neither land nor water and where venomous reptiles struck several guards. We had no knowledge of how to help them. They died in agony.

We entered high plains with verdant pastures and running streams, surrounded by clusters of towering trees. We began our ascent into tall mountains whose tops were often covered in the clouds. It was cold. We killed game for food and clothing. We came upon a raging river deep in a steep gorge, fed by a magnificent waterfall, which spit forth a torrent of water from the mountains. We were soaked with freezing water by the blinding spray. We followed the river downstream for three days before we found a place to ford the river. With severe difficulty, the queen and most of us crossed the river. Several of our slaves, mourners, and soldiers were killed by the large lizard-like reptiles who lived in this river. Several days later we stumbled upon this small valley hidden between towering mountains. That night we saw that the rocks near the base of the smaller mountain glowed with an eerie green light. On inspection, we saw a small opening that seemed to lead to the interior of the mountain. Our slaves enlarged the opening. Entering I found a small grotto. The walls glowed in a soft green light as if lit by a full moon. We performed the burial ritual and put the queen to rest in her homeland. Slaves closed the opening and we planted trees to cover it. The trees died quickly. Our astrologer reckoned that we had traveled almost one year. To regain our strength and to provision our group we stayed in this valley for many days. Soon many in our party became sick with a strange illness. Our physician was befuddled. The hands of the slaves who dug to open the grotto emitted this strange light. They died soon. Many of the guard and mourners lost their hair. They could not eat or drink. They also died. We were so few we could not bury the many dead. I fear that I cannot return to my home in Jerusalem. I also am sick.

Boaz.

THE ARMISTICE

This story is not about the Armistice of the eleventh hour, of the eleventh day, of the eleventh month in 1918 at Versailles. Rather it's the July 27 1953 Armistice at Panmunjom, Korea. After 25 months of fighting, including a year's stalemate that neither side could exploit, the Communist North Koreans and Chinese agreed to a cease fire with the United Nations forces, valid for only 90 days. The stalemate left the Korean peninsula divided just about where the war started on June 25, 1950—along the 38th North Parallel.

This narrative is true—well almost true. I'm a retired sailor. And, as sailors we are wont to occasionally expand, distort, and fabricate events. Not often, mind you, but enough for you to read the following story with a critical eye.

We were at the United Nations Base Camp at Munsan-Ni, Korea. It was late-October, 1953. Hostilities had ceased. The Prisoners-of-War (POWs) on both sides had been exchanged. Our task: to mill about smartly awaiting orders to go somewhere and photograph something or to document hostilities should the North Koreans and Chinese Communists not honor the cease fire after ninety days.

Throughout this Korean War the US Navy's Pacific Fleet Combat Camera Group supported the First Marine Division with motion picture and still photography. I'm a sailor. Not had any combat training. I knew squat about Marine arms.

We also supported the United Nations Contingent that was negotiating peace talks at Pan-Mun-Jom with the Communists. Please note: the Korean

War was not a "Police Action" as President Harry Truman dubbed it—some 37,000 GI were killed in Korea, 103,000 wounded.

We were skeptical that the North Koreans and Red Chinese would honor our proposal to extend the Armistice after ninety days. Accordingly, early on the morning of 25 October, our Leading Chief, Charles Terry, tasked Ken Giles and me to get to the Marine's 3rd infantry battalion on "Outpost Boston" just on the United Nation's side of the Demilitarized Zone (DMZ) and photograph "…whatever happens the next few days."

Photographer's Mate, S. Martin Shelton

We hooked up with a platoon of Marines in the Third regiment. I carried a Colt 45, the 1911 model, for defense. Got the Lance Corporal to check me out on the Browning Automatic Rifle (BAR)—just in case, and photoed Marines preparing for the expected Red onslaught. I climbed the watchtower and peered at the Chinese through powerful binoculars as they prepared defensive positions. The night of the 26th the Reds, across the DMZ, made a terrible racket but did not move out of their positions. Noting of note happened on the 27th. Camped out with these Marines for a couple of more days. The cease fire held. For now, I reckon the Red Koreans and Chinese were content with the Armistice deal.

Back at Base Camp, not much was going on. In fact, the US Army was beginning to close it down as the United Nations folks drifted away. Late October, we could feel winter approaching. At night, heavy sleeping bags were in order. One night about 2300 (11:00 PM for you civilians) Chief Terry rousted Johnny Hoyt and me from our sleeping bags. He told us to head for Inchon to photograph the French Foreign Legion leaving Korea and their activities in Saigon in French Indochina. We did.

The next morning, the Legionnaires boarded the USNS ship *General W. M. Black*—destined for Saigon. This contingent was needed to bolster the French's flagging war against the Communist led Viet-minh in Indochina. We presented our orders to the Officer of the Deck (OOD) for permission to board and sail. He was perplexed. Our orders were signed personally by the Commander-in-Charge, Pacific Fleet (CINCPACFLT), a four-star Admiral. They were only two lines long. As best I can remember they said, "….proceed throughout the Pacific Fleet to photograph Navy and Marine Corps activities in which you have been *verbally instructed.*" (emphasis mine). We stored our gear on board and for the next seven days we photoed Legion activities. Many spoke German, remnants from the defunct Wehrmacht.

Late one afternoon we dropped anchor near the town of Dong Hoa at the mouth of the Saigon River in the Mekong River Delta. Not prudent to sail upriver to Saigon at night. The Viet-minh controlled the river at night. Next morning we weighed anchor and sailed upriver escorted by French PT boats. We were told to stay off exposed decks. Both sides of the River were infested with Viet-minh snipers. Without incident, we docked in Saigon around noon. The dock was festooned with bunting, tricolors, French military and civilian muck-a-mucks, and a drum-and bugle corps blaring its euphonious rhythm—all to welcome the Legion to French Indochina and an uncertain fate at Dien Ben Phu a few months later.

First to debark, I scampered down the gangway as soon as it was secured. Using my Bell & Howell Eyemo-Q, 35mm motion-picture camera,

I documented the scene—shooting hundreds of feet of the festivities, the Legionnaires disembarking, assembling, and taking honors. Of note, the only uniforms I had were two sets of Marine green dungarees. My Navy uniform was somewhere in Japan, I reckon.

To set the scene: I was an American GI in uniform in French Indochina—a super-big NO-NO in October, 1953. The USA was not "officially" involved in this war. Even though we had a number of our officers (aviators, intelligence types, and others) as advisors in civilian clothes with the French military—folks who had "resigned" their commission in our Armed Forces. Such delicacies were far beyond my understanding. Chief Terry said do it. And I did it.

As required, we reported to the Naval Attaché to have our orders endorsed. We finally found his office—on the second deck in a spiffy office building on Ly Thai Road. We entered and were greeted by a dazzlingly beautiful Vietnamese woman. She was Colonel Hancock's receptionist. She asked if we would please print our names on these blank white cards. We did. She carefully placed these two cards on a silver tray and glided into a rear office. In a moment or so we heard a shout, "Show those two Marines in here."

We snapped to attention in front of the Marine Colonel. In a second or so, the scene materialized. We were in a large office decorated in the style of a W. Somerset Maugham novel of the South Seas. In the corner sat a coolie pushing back and forth on a rope tied to an overhead rattan fan. The colonel, not having a combat command during the Korean War, was smoldering. Opportunity knocks, he figured. He railed that there was a lot of fighting around Dien Ben Phu. "Let's get up there and get some damn good photographs."

I explained that in fact we were sailors and not Marines, just down from Korea and bound for Japan. He didn't care. We were American servicemen photographers in his office. "Let's go!" Not having a death wish and realizing that, in any case, we weren't supposed to be there, I told the Colonel that we were out of film, and had to return to Japan on the *Black*. To seal the deal, I promised him that we'd send some Navy photographers as soon as we got back. (Sailors don't fib.)

We spend the next several days fotoing activities in and around Saigon. Got aboard the *Black* and sailed to Japan. End of story? Not quite. As luck would have it, a French photographer for the newspaper *Le Figaro* snapped a photo of the Legionnaires debarking. A few days later this foto was published in *Le Figaro* in Paris. And there I was clearly visible on the Saigon dock in my American uniform.. Big time "el stinko" with State Department, Department of Defense, etc. Fortunately, my Commanding Officer, Lieutenant Commander (Lcdr) Thad Odell, held the hounds at bay. He congratulated Hoyt and me for an outstanding job—as did the State Department in a SECRET message. Lcdr Odell's official response to the hubbub was, "We weren't there."

ALPINE

I was on the feeder road to Alpine, about thirty miles south of Interstate I-10. The flashing red-light on my instrument panel caught my eye, "Coolant low. Stop Vehicle." Ugh! Sure pal. Anytime. Here I am in the middle of the Sonoran Desert on a blistering hot day in mid-July; and I'm supposed to pull over, shut down my Volvo, and wait for a Good Samaritan to happen by on this out-of-the-way road with a container of coolant to give me. Sure! I also believe in the tooth fairy.

Evaluating the options, I decided to push on; Alpine is only fifty miles down the road. I reckoned that there ought to be a reserve supply of coolant—as most modern-day automobiles have. Resolved, I hit the starter, pushed the gear lever into "Drive" and pressed on at a reduced speed. About ten miles down the road, I began to hear a grinding noise. It grew louder and louder, and in a few minutes, my engine froze, my transmission ground to small metallic particles, and my Volvo lurched to a hard stop. The radiator cap flew off, and what was left of the coolant spewed upward like a geyser.

Damn. And, double damn. My only option is to wait for someone in an automobile, wagon, or a horse to come by and give me a lift.

Praise the Lord! In just a few minutes a flaming red Porsche convertible sped by going lickety-split. As best I could see, a female was driving. She didn't even slow down. "I snapped a formal salute and shouted contemptuously after the rapidly receding convertible, 'Thanks a lot, hot-shot.'" By some mysterious hand, she must have had a change of heart. She whipped that Porsche around on a dime, sped back to my Volvo, screeched to a stop, leaned out over the window, and with that big-tooth smile purred, "Need a ride, big boy?"

Now let me tell you, I've seen beautiful, sexy, and flirtatious dames before, but this female was the acme of feminine pulchritude—what every young fellow dreams about: long blonde hair cascading down her head to frame a face that would launch a thousand ships. She was tall and willowy, with long legs and a curvy figure that men would covet. Her eyes were large, smoke-blue, set wide apart, and looked inviting. High cheek bones, full painted lips that beckoned to be kissed, a Roman nose with just a slight up-turn. She wore a light powder-blue sun suit that was designed to fit very tight and expose more than it ought.

"Yes indeed, I need to get to Alpine."

"She smiled wickedly. "Tough, cowboy. No deal. If you were a female ready for a good time you'd be in." She sped off and gave me the middle-finger salute.

HAWAII CLIPPER

A *roman à clef*

Captain Leonard Terletzky leans out of the cockpit window and shouts to the steward standing in the forward hatch, "Cast off the bow line."

"Aye, aye, Sir." There is a faint water splash. "Clear."

It's 0608 hours, 29 July 1938. Terletzky deftly maneuvers the giant Pan American World Airways Martin M-130 flying boat into the main channel in Apra Harbor, Guam. He eases the throttles forward, the four Pratt & Whitney Twin Wasp, 16 cylinder, 950 horsepower engines roar thunderously, and the *Hawaii Clipper* skims across the placid water of Apra Harbor, leaving a whale-like rooster tail. Forty-five seconds later, the aircraft breaks the suction holding it to the sea and is airborne—foamy water streams off its hull. Hundreds of people line the quay to watch the takeoff and the ship's graceful climb-out. Its destination is Manila, about 1,400 nautical miles and twelve hours flying time away.

History records this as the last time anyone saw the *Hawaii Clipper*.

Martin Model C, China Clipper

James L. Weldon, Director of the Civil Aeronautics Board, has tasked me, Captain Edward Reilly, with leading the investigation into the disappearance of Pan American World Airways aircraft registration number NC 14714 and radio call sign KHAZB.

Here's a summary of the facts surrounding the disappearance of the *Hawaii Clipper*. This aircraft was two years old. Three months ago, certified technicians conducted a comprehensive check on this aircraft, including its four engines. It passed with only minor interior, cosmetic deficiencies, which were fixed promptly. The ship was in tiptop mechanical and structural condition when it lifted off from Apra Harbor.

Every half-hour, William McCarty, the Flight Radio Operator and Navigator, transmitted to Manila and Guam a position report and weather conditions. His last report, at noon, was routine: "Altitude 9,100 feet, ground speed 112 knots, scattered rain, and cumulus clouds with tops at 9,200 feet." At the time, the *Hawaii Clipper* was about 680 nautical miles out from Manila.

During the next several minutes, Eduardo Fernandez, radio operator at Radio Panay (Manila), tried to raise the *Hawaii Clipper*—to no avail. His numerous radio requests for information over the following ninety minutes went unanswered. At 1330 hours, Pan American officials in Manila declared the *Hawaii Clipper* missing and broadcast the distress call on 121.5 megacycles to all stations. This distress call was repeated every five minutes for twenty-four hours.

The U.S. Army transport ship *SS Megis* was in the area of the *Hawaii Clipper's* last reported position. Its captain changed course to reach the clipper's last position and began a search. By early the next morning, the U.S. Navy had dispatched a task force of ten destroyers, five submarines, and several Consolidated PBY Catalina long-range patrol aircraft. On August 5th, after eight days of extensive searching, Pan American World Airways and the U.S. Navy cancelled all search operations. In summary, there was no trace of the *Hawaii Clipper*—no oil slick, no debris, no bodies, nothing.

I've studied every conceivable angle of this tragic scenario. It's baffling. How could the huge *Hawaii Clipper,* with a crew of nine and twelve passengers, disappear without a trace? It's near impossible. Every aircraft accident at sea leaves some sort of trace—oil, most certainly. Sometimes the oil will remain on the surface for many days.

If the *Clipper* were in trouble, William McCarty, the Flight Radio Operator, would have broadcast distress signals "May Day" and "SOS." He would have answered Radio Panay with their position, type of trouble, and intentions. Even if the radio were out of commission, they had mechanical devices to use if the clipper were on the ocean: flares, flags, and dyes.

Another scenario I considered is a catastrophic disaster of some sort: a lightning strike that destroyed the electronics or caused a complete structural failure of some critical component—not likely, because of the non-threatening weather. Engine failure: if two engines had failed, the remaining two Twin Wasp engines would have kept the clipper flying.

An untoward scenario is that a Japanese aircraft shot down the clipper. It was flying close to the Japanese-controlled Mandated Islands that were enshrouded in military secrecy. Nonetheless, any catastrophic scenario would leave debris on the ocean's surface.

In my report to the Civil Aeronautics Board, I concluded that there is no credible evidence to explain the *Hawaii Clipper's* disappearance. It's an unfathomable mystery.

In fact, I have no evidence, credible or circumstantial, about this aircraft enigma. However, several disparate facts regarding four passengers have engendered further research.

Out of Guam, there were twelve passengers on the *Hawaii Clipper.* The four of interest are:

Mister Edward E. Wyman, vice president of sales for the Curtis Wright Aeronautical Corporation, New York. He was en route to Chunking to meet with Generalissimo Chiang Kai-shek to conclude a deal for twenty-four Curtiss P-40 Tomahawk pursuit airplanes—the latest and finest in the United States' arsenal.

Mister Choy Wah-sun, a wealthy entrepreneur from New Jersey en route to Hong Kong to deliver three million dollars in gold certificates to General Li Tung-jin of the Nationalist Chinese Air Force to purchase the P-40s.

Countess Magdalena Makarenko, an enchanting White Russian *émigré* and an international adventuress with no known permanent residence or bank account. She boarded the *Hawaii Clipper* in Alameda, California, and paid cash for her ticket to Manila. Based on meager bits of information from the FBI, and rumor, I surmise that she was in the employ of the Japanese Black Dragon Society—the Japanese *unofficial* intelligence organization.

Mister Itoi Hakubumi, Japanese consul general for San Francisco, traveling with diplomatic immunity. In his previous posting, he was the staff intelligence officer for the Japanese Kwangtung Army. The FBI disclosed that he is a Lieutenant Colonel in the Black Dragon Society.

Here's a scenario I've concocted that would explain the *Hawaii Clipper's* mysterious disappearance. Mister Kaishou Tanaka, a student at San Francisco State University, a part-time clerk at the Pan American World Airways desk in San Francisco, and a sleeper agent for Japanese intelligence, used a one-time pad to pass the passenger list to Ito Hakubumi. Immediately, Hakubumi recognized the implications and sent a coded cable via the RCA network to Mister Hirako Takamura in Tokyo. He was the director of the Kempeitai, the Japanese secret police, and controller of the Black Dragon Society. Takamura's orders were to take whatever actions needed to prevent those millions of dollars from reaching China, and to foil the shipment of Curtis Wright P-40 aircrafts to Chunking. (Note: In 1938, China and Japan were engaged in a ruthless war.)

Ito Hakubumi's first task was to order Magdalena Makarenko to seduce Edward E. Wyman to get the details of the pursuit airplane transfer to China. Magdalena devised a "cute meet" with Wyman and enticed him to join her in a toast at the Top of the Mark's cocktail lounge. Several Mai Tais later, the pair was in Wyman's room. She spiked his next drink with chloral hydrate—knockout drops. Shortly, she was riffling through his valise and found the information.

The *Hawaii Clipper* was flying in a smooth sky. It was shortly after noon and the steward was serving lunch. Ito Hakubumi rose and walked into the cockpit. He asked William McCarty about their position and their ground speed. Not suspecting anything untoward, perhaps accepting the question as just idle curiosity, McCarty gave Hakubumi the information.

Magdalena Makarenko, seeing Hakubumi go into the cockpit and not return, knew that she had to execute the second phase of her mission. She withdrew a pistol from her handbag and forced the steward, Ivan Parker, into a closet in the rear of the aircraft. After snapping the lock, she raced to the front of the passenger compartment and shouted, "Everyone remain calm and remain in your seats. The Japanese Black Dragon Society has commandeered this airplane. No one will be hurt if you do not interfere."

Hakubumi fired three times into the radios, rendering them useless, put his pistol to Captain Terletzky's head, and ordered him to turn south and head for the Japanese Naval Base on Palau Island in the Caroline Islands— about 600 nautical miles south. He demanded that McCarty plot the course. Having never trained for or experienced a highjacking, the crew had no options to thwart it. Accordingly, they complied obediently. In the passenger compartment, Makarenko and her pistol had complete control. The passengers grumbled but remained passive—some continued their lunch.

Five hours later, Hakubumi commanded Captain Terletzky to drop to an altitude of one thousand feet and maintain course. Soon, on the horizon, Hakubumi spotted the Imperial Japanese seaplane tender *IJN Akistusima*, about three nautical miles north of Palau. He forced Terletzky to land and taxi toward the tender. Fortunately, the sea was calm.

Please note: U.S. naval intelligence had positive confirmation that the *IJN Akistusima* was in the Mandated Caroline Islands on 29 July 1938. I'll continue my theoretical narrative of this true mysterious disappearance of Pan American Flight *Hawaii Clipper*. However, I have no evidence to support it—it's best-guess speculation. (Dear readers, what ending would you devise?)

Japanese marines forced the passengers and crew on board the *IJN Akistusima*. The captain sent a boarding party aboard the *Hawaii Clipper* to recover the three million dollars in U.S. gold certificates and other items of value or interest. With his boarding party back aboard, the captain eased his ship away from the *Hawaii Clipper*. At one-hundred meters distant, the marines raked it with a pair of 127 mm deck guns. Tracers from small-arms fire set the remaining gasoline and engine oil on fire. Within a few minutes, the *Clipper* slipped below the surface, and the burning gasoline and oil soon left no evidence. There was no trace of the *Hawaii Clipper*.

The passengers and crew, including Magdalena Makarenko, were herded to the fantail and the marines opened fire with machine guns. Their bodies were dumped into the shark-infested sea.

Afterword

During the 1945 battle for Manila, Brigadier General Ito Hakubumi was the staff intelligence officer for General Tomoyuki Yamashita, commander of the Imperial Japanese Army in the Philippines. Hakubumi was instrumental in fostering the Rape of Manila, the atrocity in which frenzied Japanese marines and soldiers murdered approximately 50,000 Filipino civilians. Ito Hakubumi was tried as a war criminal, convicted, and hung on 23 February 1946.

THE REGICIDE

Kremlin, Moscow

16 July 1918

Vladimir Ilyich Lenin is at his desk writing with an intense focus. He wears a grey suit with a scarlet tie over his off-white shirt. It is a dark afternoon that matches the dull grey of his suit and office. On the walls are photographs and posters extolling the virtues of collectivism.

Lenin, the leader of the Russian Revolution, is now the Chairman of the People's Commissars of the Union of Soviet Socialist Republics. He is fifty-eight years old, bald, with a full mustache and a Van Dyke beard. His deep brown eyes are alive with passionate fervor.

Vladimir Ilyich Lenin

He writes with slow precision on a paper bearing the official seal of the Union of Soviet Socialist Republics government—the hammer and sickle in yellow on a red background. Finished, he stows the pen, lifts the paper in his left hand, leans back in his chair, and meticulously reads the document. He reads it again. A faint smile spreads over his face.

Satisfied, he hands it to Felix Dzerzhinsky, the ruthless leader of Lenin's secret police, the "Cheka." He is exactly the kind of unbridled sociopath that Lenin wants as his lead henchman. Dzerzhinsky is a medium-sized man with a brown, stony face and a fixed expression. He wears a walrus mustache and a short, pointed, Van Dyke beard. Lenin leans forward and dictates, "Read it, Felix. Read it out loud. I want to hear how it sounds. I want the world to hear it. Read it now!"

Dzerzhinsky looks mildly interested as he begins to read the short note. Now, seriously interested, he reads it again, then once again. He looks up from the document to Lenin and tentatively asks him, "You are positive that this is the correct action at this time?"

Lenin frowns in response. "Of course I'm sure."

Dzerzhinsky, with a mild retort, suggests, "Comrade, my point is, I wonder if it would not be prudent to wait until we have consolidated more control over the country. Our political and military positions are still in flux."

Lenin snaps, "Comrade Dzerzhinsky, you keep the Cheka working to eliminate the counter-revolutionaries and I will lead our socialist country." Irritated, he shifts in his chair, then picks up the pen and taps it on his desk. He stares blankly out a window as the Kremlin glows scarlet in the dusk. Clearly, he is evaluating Dzerzhinsky's comments because they have a ring of truth. The tap, tap, tap of the pen continues. Lenin puzzles over the scarlet sunset. Is it an omen—red for Red?

After a minute or so, he shifts in his chair to face Grigory Zinoviev, the third man in the room. Lenin holds him in a thoughtful gaze for a few moments, then says in a spirited voice, "Let us hear what Comrade Zinoviev has to say."

Dzerzhinsky turns to Grigory and hands him the document. Zinoviev, a revolutionary who is now the Interior Minister, is a close confidant of Lenin.

Zinoviev is a big brute of a man with icy blue eyes and long midnight-black hair. His face is littered with smallpox scars, but he is clean-shaven—almost proud of his disfigurement.

After a brief pause and in a gruff, bass voice, Zinoviev responds, "My respects, Comrade Lenin, but I ask you to reconsider. The majority of the proletariat still love their Czar, who is also the spiritual leader of the Orthodox Church. Such an audacious action will cause many loyal proletariat to question your motives. I do not recommend this precipitous order. Over the next few months, let us reflect on some of the alternatives."

Lenin shouts, "Stop! Stop it, Zinoviev. Am I surrounded by naysayers? The Communist Party and the Third International Congress of Soviets made me Party Chairman and Head of State. I know what is best for our Soviet Union. The peasants will do as the State directs."

Zinoviev, who has remained standing, straightens his shoulders and responds deferentially, yet with conviction, "If you insist on this course of action, our socialist government will be in extreme peril and may well fall to the Western imperialists. We are fighting them on five fronts. The White Armies of General Denikin and Admiral Kolchak defeat our Red Army in every engagement. Our desertion rates are excessively high. The Northern Russian Expedition of fourteen battalions of British Commonwealth, American, and French colonial troops has occupied Murmansk and Archangel, and they are advancing into the interior."

Lenin is clearly annoyed that his old friend should question his judgment. He rises from his chair, glares at Zinoviev, shakes his closed fist at him, and snaps, "The Soviet Union will prevail over these Western interlopers. Our allies—the sharp winter and the vast steppes—ultimately will engulf and destroy them."

Zinoviev, stunned by Lenin's sharp rebuke, looks to Dzerzhinsky for support. Dzerzhinsky looks away and shakes his head from side to side. Then he says, "Comrade Lenin has made his decision. I manage the Cheka on his authority."

Realizing that he is alone in this discussion, Zinoviev counters, "Comrade Lenin, we have been together for years. Please do not dismiss my report with such a cavalier comment, or underestimate the seriousness of these Westerners on our soil. Hear me out."

Lenin, still irritated, returns to his chair, and says, "Speak your piece, Grigory."

"There is more. American and Japanese troops have occupied Vladivostok, and the Japanese are moving up the peninsula and assembling at our border with Mongolia near Nomonhan. They have occupied all of Sakhalin Island. The Japanese are continuing the war of 1904 unopposed, in violation of the Treaty of Portsmouth. British and Indian troops have invaded the Southern Caucasus. And perhaps most important, the Czech Legion has control of the Trans-Siberian Railroad from Kazan to Novosibirsk."

Lenin snaps, "Your point, Comrade? Make it. I have a country to rule."

Zinoviev responds forcefully, "Comrade Lenin, my point is critical. We cannot defeat them all. We are isolated from the rest of the world. If our socialist government is to survive we must have peace—peace at any cost. We do not need more armed hostility. We need Western recognition and wheat, lots of wheat, if we are to survive this winter. I implore you to reconsider."

"Zinoviev, you were my loyal ally in our Bolshevik Revolution that overthrew the Czar and his imperialist lackeys. Remain loyal to me now. Read my telegram. Read it out loud." demands Lenin.

With trepidation Zinoviev whispers, "Your telegram is headed Top Secret. It reads: 'To Comrade Major Vasili Yurovsky, Commanding Officer, Cheka, Ekaterinburg. No later than tomorrow evening, you are to execute the prisoners held in the Ipatiev House. Specifically, I name the Romanov royal family of Imperial Russia: the Czar Nicholas, Empress Alexandra, Czarevich Nicholas, and the Grand Duchesses Marie, Olga, Tatiana, and Anastasia. Confirm results. Signed, Lenin."

"Give this telegram to Comrade Roman Malinovsky, our new Commissar of Posts and Telegraphs. Have him encrypt it in our Omega code for immediate transmission."

*Czar Nicholas II, Empress Alexandra, and
Children: Olga, Tatiana, Marie, Anastasia,
and Czarevich Nicholas*

Ipatiev House, Ekaterinburg, Siberia, 17 July 1918

The corner windows in the second story are lit in the Ipatiev House, an elegant two-story dacha situated on several hundred acres of well-tended gardens, fountains, ponds, and virgin birch forest. The Bolsheviks have dubbed this dacha "The House of Special Purpose." It is shortly before midnight, but the house is astir with activity.

The Imperial Romanov family have been prisoners of the Cheka in this house since April, closely confined and daily suffering the insults of their Red guards. Their only comfort is the fact that they are together. Rumors of impending rescue reach them periodically, but each time they wait in vain.

This evening, the family calmly retire at the usual time. About an hour later, the sergeant of the guard rouses them and orders them to dress and hurry downstairs to the cellar. He explains that the Czech Legion and a unit of the White Army are approaching Ekaterinburg, and the Regional Soviet has ordered that they be moved.

The family rush to dress and pack a few personal belongings. When the family arrive in the cellar, the sergeant tells them that their transportation will arrive shortly. A Cheka guard brings a chair for the Empress. For a moment, Alexandra's heart fills with hope. If the Czech Legion and White Army are so near, rescue is imminent. Soon the family will be together, free of these horrid Bolsheviks, and en route to Great Britain. She puts an arm around her youngest daughter Anastasia's waist. Thanks be to God.

Suddenly, a squad of Cheka soldiers with their rifles at port arms marches single file and at double time into the cellar. After the last soldier is in position, the first sergeant commands, "Squad, halt! Right face." The soldiers turn to face the Romanovs. After a moment, the sergeant shouts, "Squad, ah-ten-hut!" The sound of rifle butts hitting the concrete floor reverberates throughout the cellar.

Major Vasili Yurovsky

Several minutes later, Major Vasili Yurovsky enters. He is the senior Cheka officer in the area. He wears the summer grey, short-sleeved, tunic uniform with red piping, and his major's pips on the shoulder boards.

"Present. Arms!" commands the first sergeant.

The soldiers bring their rifles to the present-arms position to salute their commanding officer.

In return, Major Yurovsky returns a snappy hand salute.

The Czarevich giggles in delight at the military prompt.

However, fear races through the rest of the Romanov family as they wonder what this military demonstration has to do with their rescue.

"Order arms!" commands the sergeant. The soldiers return their rifles to their right sides. The pounding rifle butts hitting the concrete floor send chills through the Romanovs.

Yurovsky orders Alexandra to stand. The indignity of this crass Bolshevik officer ordering the Empress of All the Russias to comply with his command is unthinkable. She stares with smoldering hostility at Yurovsky. But, no longer enjoying the resources of royal status, she complies.

With his arms akimbo, Yurovsky walks down the line of the imperial family. He stops in front of each person and looks intently into his or her eyes. All but the Empress turn away from him. Summoning all her courage, she returns her most imperious glower of disdain. He smiles faintly at her feeble attempt at bravado.

The Czarevich is dressed in his sailor uniform. Maintaining proper military protocol, he salutes Yurovsky. The major stares at him contemptuously and does not return the salute.

Extreme apprehension engulfs daughters Maria, Tatiana, Olga, and Anastasia. Unsure of what is happening and fearing the worst, they cannot control their fear and sob softly.

Major Yurovsky turns to the first sergeant and snaps, "On my orders!"

"As you say. Sir!"

Yurovsky moves to the concrete steps and climbs three. "Port arms!" he shouts. He surveys the scene to ensure that the Romanovs are positioned correctly and that his soldiers are ready.

Satisfied that the staging is correct, Yurovsky commands, "Fix bayonets!"

There is a loud clanging of metal as the soldiers snap their bayonets onto their rifles.

The Romanovs now understand with crystal clarity that they are not going to be rescued. Death is their fate. The Bolsheviks will assassinate them—one and all. Alexandra stands erect and defiant. The Czar seems to be in a daze. Their daughters fight to be brave and to hold back her fearful tears.

"Load!" The soldiers pull back the bolts of their rifles, and then jam them forward, loading a round into the rifles' chambers. The metal-on-metal clicking sends a vibration of horror through the cellar.

Unable to control their fear, the daughters begin to sob and make the sign of the cross. Alexandra commands, "Be brave. You are Romanovs. Saint Nicholas will guide you."

The Czar has been standing silently, as if he were in a dream. Aroused by the loud clicking of metal, he exclaims, "What!"

"Aim!" The riflemen select the nearest target.

Cries. Screams.

"Fire."

The deafening thunder of the first volley reverberates through the cellar. Agonized screams. Another volley. Another. And another. Silence.

Major Yurovsky cannot see clearly in the small, smoke-filled cellar. He checks the mutilated human forms askew on the concrete floor. There are no heartbeats. There is no light in any of the eyes. He grimaces at the bloody corpses. Even for a hardened Cheka officer, the scene is gruesome. The cellar window goes dark.

Afterwards
Moscow, 30 September 1938

The Minister of Justice of the Union of Soviet Socialist Republics released a statement today that said, "Laverenti Bera, Head of the People's Commissariat for Internal Affairs, the NKVD, has charged Colonel General Yaakov Yurovsky with Anti-Soviet Activities."

"This morning Colonel General Yurovsky was tried, convicted, and executed at Lubyanka prison."

SOUTHERN PACIFIC

Hank was snake bit. I don't mean figuratively, but literally. That southern pacific rattlesnake hit him on the right calf. He yelled. I was about 20 feet away photographing a well-preserved ol'-time cabin. As I got to Hank I saw the reptile slither away. That fellow was over five feet long—a big bastard. Snapped his foto. Hank was down, in serious pain, and in deep trouble. The Southern Pacific rattler is a seriously dangerous reptile. It injects a dual-dose venom that attacks both the cardiovascular and the neurological systems.

Southern Pacific Rattlesnake

We were on our annual photographic ghost town trip. This year we were operating in the Black Mountains in the remote southern section of Death Valley National Park. Folks don't venture here much—not touristy. We were at the Gold Valley site—an oasis nestled in a small hollow about halfway up the mountain. It's an outstanding site with seven intact wood structures.

A hidden spring in tall salt grass nestled aside the mountain that nurtures this oasis, several palm trees, birds galore, rabbits, and other critters. The cabins are on the southern periphery of the oasis in a small flat. Well worth the eight-mile, serious four-wheel drive up the mountain trail. It was a bright clear autumn day with the sun low on the horizon—making bold shadows that enhanced depth in our photos.

A few minutes earlier, Hank said that he was going into the oasis to find and photograph the spring. Concentrating on my photography, it took me a second or so for Hank's comment to register. Being a seasoned ghost-towner, I shouted, "Don't go. Dumb idea. That salt grass is high." Too late. He was about ten feet into the grass.

The southern pacific rattler was lying in wait alongside an animal trail in the tall grass. watching for a rabbit or a squirrel to wander by—its dinner. Hank shouted, "I'm hit." He yelled in pain. "I'm rattlesnake bit." He hobbled toward me. His right hand holding his calf tight. "Heard the buzz too late. Step right on top of that damn reptile. It bit me almost instantaneously."

Clearly the situation was critical. Fast action essential. Recalling the current medical advice on snakebite. No first aid: no tourniquet, no incisions at the bite to suck out the venom, no booze. No nothing except water. Get the patient to medical help post haste.

Hank wasn't doing so well—mumbling incoherently, sweating profusely, and labored breathing. I helped him into our truck. Strapped him in the passenger's seat. Ran around to the driver's side. Then I spotted it. Our left rear tire was flat. Damn! (And other invectives) I had lots of experience changing flat tires on this type of truck, should take less than 15 minutes. Did I mention that we were in a rental truck? No need to mess up our own equipment.

The spare tire was tucked under the fold-down door in the rear. Got the wheel-changing equipment. Knelt to start cranking down the spare. Double damn!! It was fastened solid to the holding frame with the biggest padlock I'd ever seen. Had no key. Rental agent failed to mention this major detail, and we had no bolt cutter. (An essential survival tool on all ghost town trips.)

Time for action. Started broadcasting on channel 9 on my Citizen's Band radio. Transmitted the "May Day," "May Day," "May Day" signals for several minutes. No response. Just gibberish on the channel. Not one voice as such, but a zillion voices atop one another—pure noise. Should be a clear channel for emergencies only. Tried 911 on my cell phone. No response. Tried the rental agency. No response. Surrounded by mountains in this small hollow, there was no line-of-sight for my signal to be broadcast into the ether. Not smart to wait for a tourist or a ranger to show. This remote site is just too tough to navigate and too far from civilization.

Only several minutes since that rattler bit Hank. He was semi-conscious. Uneven breathing. Spittle oozing from his mouth. Moaning faintly. Decision time. No option but to drive on the flat tire. Turned the key. Jammed the drive lever into four-wheel drive. Punched the gasoline peddle and we were moving.

Eight miles of miserable four-wheel driving. Wow! What a drive. Hit damn near every boulder on this craggy, twisting mountain trail. "Rough" doesn't begin to describe the bouncing drive. On the rebound, of a particularly severe bounce, the front axel ripped a semi-buried boulder out of the ground—making a terrible racket as it bounced around the rear of the trick. Knocked the hood open. Froze the fan. Suspect that the engine mounts were knocked loose. No telling the damage to the mechanisms on the underside of the truck. Actually, it was a quick fix for the fan—reset several bolts. Wired the hood closed, and to my surprise, we got underway. Nonetheless with severe vibration and clunking. But we were moving. Don't know if Hank was aware of the rough ride.

Reckon I was a little heavy-footed on the gas pedal, but Hank didn't look too good. Before long the flat tire was worn through and its remains spun into the desert. Now, riding on the rim. Sparks flying. Difficult to steer. Making progress, though. Just a few miles to the black top. "Coyote, get off the road—we're coming through." We made it.

Got to Shoshone—a burg on highway number 127—just southeast of the Park's boundary. Pulled into the lone service station. Let me rephrase that last sentence, "Our truck limped into the lone service station, then expired."

Hank was not moving. Breathing much labored. Got a pulse, but weak. His face seemed frozen—paralysis probably. At least he's not feverish. Seemed cool to my touch—blood pressure down.

Manager at the two-pump service station punched in "911" on his landline phone. Got the emergency operator in Las Vegas. Medical helicopter en route. I tried to keep Hank comfortable—best I could. Hate waiting. Impatience is my cross.

After an eternity, that big bird landed on the blacktop. EMTs got Hank, did their examination, and gave him a shot of something—adrenaline? On the gurney and into the chopper, Hank's gone to Las Vegas. Great theatrical shows. Scantily clad showgirls (or is "women" nowadays?). Fancy food in gigantic buffets. How 'bout the Emergency Room at the University Medical Center. "Good luck, pal."

I walked around the truck. The rear wheel worn down to a hub, bent, distorted, and otherwise a mess. Steam gushing from the radiator. Oil spewing on the asphalt. Reckon the axel, engine, transmission, and lots of parts on that wreck needed fixing. Durable truck. "Thanks for the life-saving ride. See ya in the junk yard."

I called the auto-rental office in Vegas. Told the desk clerk the story. She was taken aback—never had this sort of report. Said she'd send the wrecker for the remains of the truck. Wonder if my insurance will cover the damage if I am responsible. Find out later. I unloaded our stuff—lots of it—survival gear, food stores, water, soft drinks, grips, navigation paraphernalia, maps, log books, and our camera equipment. Manager let me stow our gear in the back of his station. I hitched a ride to Vegas with the next traveler heading south that stopped at the station. Checked into a motel off the strip. Got to the hospital 'round midnight.

Hank was in Intensive Care. Unconscious. White-clad folks hovering about. Senior medico said. "It will be me a miracle if the patient survives."

"Double damn." *Those large fangs on that monster reptile injected Hank with a super dose of neurotoxin and neurological venom.* Fortunately, the hospital had the specific antivenin serum for the southern pacific rattlesnake.

Next afternoon, Hank was stable. Still "big-time" ailing. "Prognosis is tentative." Will be a day or so before we know with certainty. Counting on positive. Following day, it was.

Rented an automobile from the rental agency. As luck would have it, the clerk was the one I talked with about the truck. Not happy. Said there was so much damage to that truck that it is being sold for scrap. The engine, transmission and most all other moving parts were "kaput." Must have knocked off the oil pan on my hasty trip down the mountain. No oil—no engine.

Spent the few days in Vegas—most of time at the hospital. No shows and no showgirls—shucks. A several sumptuous buffets, however. Imbibing adult beverages in the evening with prudence. Watched lots of old movies on the TV. *Casablanca* and *The Maltese Falcon* are my favorites.

Hank steadily improved. With all the drugs roiling his body, he had a difficult time focusing on reality. Two days later, he could talk with semi-coherence. Doesn't remember much. The following days, I relayed the events in small doses. Steadily improving. On the seventh day the medicos released him. We went to Shoshone to recover our gear. Left a case of Wild Turkey, 101 proof, for the station manager. Went home.

For the next few weeks I was consumed with revenge on that southern pacific *bastardo*. One evening, after several jiggers of rye, I devised a plan. I'm going to Gold Valley. Burn that brush and palm trees to a cinder. And, with a clear view of the oasis, I would blast every damn reptile with my Mossberg 12 gauge.

With the morning comes light (and a sore head). Not a topnotch idea. Gold Valley is in a national park. And park rangers don't look kindly on such vandalism. Reckon I'd be in prison for several years. Let that damn reptile alone. It does eat rats and other vermin. A balance of nature, as it were.

I kept in touch with Hank from time to time. He walks with a cane. And will for the rest of his life. Otherwise, he's none the worse from his southern pacific adventure. As autumn approached, I asked him to go with me on a photographic ghost town trip in Colorado. He stared at me with the most incredulous expression. After a second or so he snapped, "Surely you jest."

FENWICK

Earlier this morning, Fenwick stumbled out of the Emergency Ward. His six-foot frame was bent, and quiet sobs racked his soul. His baby sister, Laura, lies dead. Earlier this morning she had been brutally raped and stabbed repeatedly. With her last breath she had murmured, "Hugo. Hugo Rawlins."

Hugo was Laura's high-school sweetheart. Nowadays, they dated from time to time as friends.

Fenwick sat in his delivery truck as rage and sorrow engulfed. Several minutes later, he gained control and carefully inserted the key, turned it and the truck roared to life. "Sis, I've just signed that bastard's death warrant."

Fenwick jams the accelerator to the floorboard. His truck lurches forward pinning his broad shoulders to the seat. Blinded with hate, his eyes narrows as he grips the steering wheel with all his 220-pound might.

The pedestrian leaps to avoid the charging truck—too late. The truck smashes into the fellow, hurling him over it and onto the street. His body lies severely contorted and blood oozes from his mouth and eyes.

Fenwick hits the brakes, turns left at the next intersection, and drives away carefully. He shouts, "Sis, I finally got that son-of-bitch! You despicable blackguard, rot in Hell." In several seconds, Fenwick regains his composure and a slow smile creeps over his face as he reflects on his morning's work. He murmurs, "Sis, rest in peace. I killed that murdering bastard. He'll not bother you anymore."

The detective bends down and turns the body over. He searches the dead man's wallet and finds his identification. He is Hugo Rawlins. Also in the wallet is a copy of an airline ticket receipt.

The chauffer of the airport limousine walks into the scene, points to the dead man, and tells the detective, "This fellow just left my limo. I picked him up at the airport about thirty-minutes ago. He was a passenger on that Acme Airlines flight from Honolulu that landed about an hour ago.

MARK GREGORY

Barcelona, Spain,

February 1937

Captain Rubio Zepeda stares at his watch as the second hand ticks incrementally to the "12." At exactly zero five hundred hours, Zepeda blows hard on his whistle three times. Mark Gregory and the other volunteer soldiers of Companies, One, Three, and Five of the Lincoln Brigade scramble out of their trenches, yell at the top of their voices, and charge towards the Falangists' defensive positions about two-hundred yards away.

Italian machine-gun fire cuts swaths through the charging soldiers, Moroccan soldiers lay down an enfilade of rifle fire, and German 88 mm artillery opens fire with a creeping barrage of deadly explosions and flying shrapnel. Within a few minutes, only a few men of the Lincoln Brigade are still moving forward. The cries of the wounded and dying increase the terrifying din.

German-88mm-Artillery GS

The Spanish Civil War is now in its second year and it envelops all of the Iberian Peninsula. The fighting is fierce and without mercy between the Marxist "Republican" government's army and the Falangists revolutionary forces of Generalissimo Francisco Franco and his Nationalist army.

Miraculously, Mark Gregory is untouched. With steely reserve, he presses forward using all his mental and physical strength. In the early morning chill, his breath forms small vapor clouds. He clears his mind of the dangerous chaos around him. His singular focus is that Moroccan trench. He grasps his Soviet Mosin Nagant rifle at port arms. The low rising sun dances off his bayonet as it sways in time to his running steps. He stumbles over a dead comrade, recovers his step, and continues his charge. Now, it's only another hundred yards to General Franco's Moroccans.

Mark Gregory is a young idealist from Dartmouth University who joined the Socialist Party of America. Believing in the righteousness of Marxism, he volunteered for the Abraham Lincoln Brigade to fight the fascists in the revolution in Spain.

It's just another fifty-yards to the Falangists' trenches. A German artillery shell explodes about a hundred feet behind the charging Mark. Shrapnel from the shell rips into his body, and the force of the explosion hurls him forward and slams him into the ground unconscious. The wounds in his legs and back bleed profusely. The intense pain forces him back to consciousness. A spasm of coughing racks his body, and he spews bright red blood. In an instant, he understands his fate. Screaming in pain, he shouts, "Am I on the true path to Marxism?"

YEN HEI LAN

St. Elizabeth's Academy for Young Ladies, Peiping, China.

10 March 1917, Morning recess

Yen Hei-lan slaps the little girl hard in the face, knocking her to the ground. A large red welt begins to form on the girl's cheek. Yen, with her legs spread apart and arms akimbo, stands over the sobbing girl, demanding that she take the ethnic slur back. Yen proclaims in an imperious voice, "Madeleine, get this through your malignant French soul, I am Chinese! Not a 'Chink'. I am not a 'slope-eyed Chink.' I am not a French colonial vassal. It is you, the pale-skinned round-eye that is the alien in the Middle Kingdom."

With hard black eyes, Yen glares at the distraught child. Occidental imperialism fuels her rage to a point that she has no voice. Screaming in her brain are the Occidental rapes of her China: unequal treaties forced on us at gunpoint, trade concessions stifling our coastal cities, and British and American gunboats patrolling the Yellow and Yangtze Rivers. Christian missionaries prostituting our ancient Confucian religion. Your opium despoiling our society.

Gasping for breath, Yen continues in a near shout, "We were a great civilization while your ancestors lived in trees. Get out of my county. My China! Get out now."

Yen Hei-lan is fourteen years old and enrolled in the exclusive St. Elizabeth's Academy for Young Ladies. She is a beautiful woman-child with large, black, daring eyes. Already her tall feminine body is fully developed into an erotic sculpture. Learned and capable far beyond her years, she is fluent in Mandarin, English, Russian, French, and Japanese.

Predominantly, her fellow students are Occidentals whose parents are from the Western embassies and corporation offices. Her classmates regard Yen Hei-lan as a loner, selfish, aggressive, and unscrupulous. Nonetheless, she is the champion athlete of the Academy—a three-goal soccer player and the captain of the tennis team.

Her only friend is an attractive, sixteen year-old Persian. The rumor among her classmates is that the Persian and Yen have a relationship that is something more intimate than just friends.

Several years ago in Anhwei Province, Yen's parents were killed in the crossfire of the savage battle between the troops of the warlord Marshal Chang Hsueh-liang and Colonel Chiang Kai-shek's Nationalist soldiers. Colonel Chiang had launched his Northwest Campaign to rout warlordism out of China. Now, Yen Hei-lan is the ward of her uncle, Wuhan Wei-kuo, who is the premier antique dealer in Peking.

Sister Mary Beatrice O'Hare, of the Sisters of Charity of Saint Elizabeth order, rushes to the aid of the fallen child. O'Hare is short and dumpy, yet she moves with speed and grace. Her rosy cheeks, deep blue eyes, and heavy brogue signal her Irish heritage. Her large white habit flaps in the wind and her long full skirt swishes loudly. She helps the fallen Madeleine to stand, wipes her tears, and consoles her with sympathetic assurances and an old-fashioned hug. She tells Madeleine, "Go to the bathroom and clean yourself. Then go to the kitchen and ask the cook to make an ice pack for your cheek. I will visit with you shortly."

She turns to Yen Hei-lan. "Miss Yen, your conduct is unacceptable. I'm appalled at your behavior. Young ladies of St. Elizabeth's do not strike anyone, no matter the provocation. We do not harangue our fellow students. We do not engage in politics. Here, we are all equally committed to academic scholarship, the social graces, and chivalrous sportsmanship. Have not these three tenets been the hallmark of your education at St. Elizabeth's?"

Yen recovers quickly from her outrage, knowing that she must be demure, because expulsion would bring shame and would ruin this singular and expensive opportunity for a nonpareil education. She feigns humility and contrition to answer Sister O'Hare's reproof. "You are correct, reverend Sister. I am shamed by my ill-advised conduct. May I suggest, however, Sister Mary Beatrice, that I was deeply wounded by the racist slur 'slope-eyed Chink' spoken by a person who just a few decades ago my ancestors would have considered barbarian."

"Yen, silence. You have done and said enough. I empathize with your hurt. Madeleine's insult is appalling and not in keeping with our protocols. I shall speak to her quite sternly. Yet no matter the provocations, our young ladies always keep self-control. We assiduously practice the etiquette of polite and genteel society—no matter the circumstances. At all times, we gracefully maintain the conventions expected of us as students and graduates of St. Elizabeth's. Is that not what we have taught, and demanded of you and all our young ladies?"

Seething inside, yet under complete external control, Yen responds, "Yes, Sister. You are correct. I have failed in my obligations to you and this esteemed school. May I beg your forgiveness?"

In a more conciliatory tone, Sister Mary Beatrice responds, "My dear Miss Yen, I do not have the power to forgive. Only a priest in the confessional, through Christ, can forgive. But I must say that I am bitterly disappointed at your behavior today. You are the brightest student in our school. You are a champion athlete, a natural leader, and mature far beyond your years. Please understand, Hei-lan, that your moral and corporal destiny will be decided by your forbearance of others, and those that offend you, and those that are not as accomplished as you. Compassion must be your counsel. Lock these prescriptions in your heart and follow them always. Is that unequivocally clear?"

"Yes, Sister. I understand and I will uphold the highest time-honored conventions of St. Elizabeth's in the future."

"Very well, Hei-lan. I accept your assurances. But there must be atonement to ease my disappointment, to make amends to Madeleine, and to reaffirm your commitment to our ideals." Knowing Hei-lan's scholarship, Sister O'Hara commands, "For your punishment for today's misconduct, you must write a letter of apology to the wounded child, and write it in French. I will review it, and if satisfactory, return it to you so that you may deliver it personally to Madeleine and make appropriate verbal atonement. Additionally, next Monday you will hand me a five-thousand-word essay written in Russian that discusses the border dispute between the Union of Soviet Socialist Republics and the Republic of China over Inner Mongolia. Include such themes as the Trans-Siberian Railroad, Japanese influence in Manchuria, and warlordism in the northwestern provinces."

"Yes, Sister. Such an assignment is appropriate for my wanton misconduct. You will have both documents Monday morning." Her thoughts, however, rage with controlled anger. *Yen Hei-lan does not capitulate to officious occidentals. These barbarians underestimate me*, she muses.

His Royal Britannic Majesty's Embassy, Peking
15 July, 1917

The military attaché, Brigadier Sir Malcolm Stanford-Brownsworth, VC, GBE, hero of the Battle of the Somme, reads the Times, Hong Kong edition. In the obituary column, he reads, "Mother Superior, Sister Mary Beatrice O'Hare, order of the Sisters of Charity, and Rector of Saint Elizabeth's Academy, has died of a mysterious illness. The physicians at St. Alphonse's Catholic Infirmary cannot diagnose the infection or explain the rapid progression of the disease. Sister O'Hara expired within two days after complaining of severe headaches. An autopsy is pending."

Indeed unfortunate, he muses. His youngest daughter, Marbella, attended St. Elizabeth's Academy and she spoke highly of Sister O'Hare. On page seven, he spots a small item: "The ten-year-old daughter of the French *Chargé d'affaires*, Madeleine de Boise, is missing. Chief Inspector Malcolm Bernard-Smyth, lead homicide detective of the International Police Force, says that there are no clues regarding her disappearance. However, from experience he suspects foul play. Enquiries are continuing."

Afterword

Dear reader, the mysterious deaths of Sister Mary Beatrice O'Hara and Madeline de Boise were never solved. Two years later, Chief Inspector Smyth transferred to the constabulary in Singapore and, after a few months, his open case files were sent to the archives, where they remained untouched.

PROFESSOR O. B. FUSCATE

Professor Fuscate's strides are long and quick. He's late for his lecture "Deconstructing Dashiell Hammett's novel *The Maltese Falcon.*" To save a few steps, he cuts through the parking lot. His mind is focused sharply on telling his students what Hammett meant in the scene where Caspar Gutman says to Sam Spade, "Yes sir, we were. But we were talking then. This is actual money, genuine coin of the realm, sir. With a dollar of this you can buy more that ten dollars of talk." A bright symbol catches the corner of his eye. He stops and spots the personalized license plate "16 CINE" on a current model Volvo sedan. His mind tries to decode the significance of this symbol. No doubt, it's an icon that reveals the automobile's owner's psyche. What is the owner's message? The conundrum piques the professor's professional pride to the degree that he must solve this riddle. Puzzled deeply, he eschews his class and resolves to deconstruct this arcane symbol.

Professor Fuscate applies his keen deductive ability to devise the owner's meaning. He immediately rationalizes that the owner of this new Volvo is astute, wealthy, socially liberal, well educated, and environmental aware. Why does the owner need to proclaim this arcane two-symbol message to the world? A boost to his ego? A protection notice? A proclamation of import? Or perhaps just a will-o'-the-wisp—but he thinks not. There is a serious message here.

First, he tackles the symbol "16." He notes that this number has no dimension: inch, volt, light-year, or furlong for examples. Nonetheless, based on the evidence and using his patented deconstruction techniques, he concluded that "16" is either a count of something or an icon that represents something known only to the owner and his cadre of cognoscenti.

License plate

He's perplexed with "CINE." He first thought is that it is an anagram in some foreign language. On reflection, he discards this idea and deconstructs this symbol as code for "SIN" and the "E" stands for "Extraordinary." With this part of the sign solved, he concludes that the owner is proclaiming his confession for sixteen major sins—all left unsaid.

Standing behind Professor Fuscate is a scruffy young fellow smoking a joint. He's wears torn jeans, wrinkled shirt, and running shoes that should have been discarded last year. He has long, shaggy hair, an unkempt beard, and emits the putrid odor of a long, unwashed body. Surprised that the professor is examining his license plate, he exhales a cloud of voluminous and odiferous smoke toward the professor. He asks, "Hey man, 'wacha doin' with my automobile?"

The professor coughs a couple of times and addresses the intruder, "I have deconstructed your license plate's symbol. He waves away some of the lingering smoke. "Pray tell young man, what are your sixteen-sins that you've proclaimed so loudly in code on you Volvo?"

Befuddled by this untoward remark, the fellow proclaims. "Ain't got no sins. And if I did, I sure ain't gonna tell you or nobody else."

"But you license plate sends the message of your sins loud and clear. Do not be ashamed. What are your discretions, if I may be so bold?"

"Professor, you ain't bold. You got a mixed up mind." He tossed his joint on the ground and exhales a volume of gray smoke that engulfs the professor. "I'm a cinema student and my personalized plate tells the world that I'm studying 16mm filmmaking.

"Quite so. Quite so. Just as I had deconstructed."

TWO GALS AND A GUY

"**Y**ep, I done it all right. I done it, but I reckon I didn't mean to. I was spittin' nails I was so angry. My evil temper got the best of me. Not that I'm an angry fella most times. But, once in a while, I jest can't stand it. I ain't got no control."

"All right, first tell me who you are and a little about your life."

"I reckon you ought ta know who I am. That's fair 'nough. Well, my name is Joshua Bob Mulroy. 'Bob,' that's short for Robert. And I live in Tonopah. That's in Nevada—'bout half way between Las Vegas and Reno."

Tonopah, Nevada

"My mama says I was born in 1880 up in Winnemucca. But I'm not sure she got that right—she was a little peculiar, don't ya know. I don't know my papa 'cause mama worked in Whiskey Pete's Chance Saloon, and she entertained the customers a bit."

"That's fine, Bob. Tell me, how do you earn a living?"

"I don't know what that's got to do with the goin' ons right now. But, I don't care much. Well, I do some hard rock mining around Silver Peak down in Esmeralda County when I set my mind to it. I got me one of them U. S. government patents for my mine. Get enough ore sometimes to keep me for a couple of months—vitals, chewin' 'bacca, and a female, now and then, at the Mustang Saloon. Other times I do some cowboying over at the Storzzi Ranch—almost in California. Don't cotton to it thet much. Too damn hard work for my tender butt. Sometimes, I do most anything to get by. Honest stuff, mostly."

"That is fine. Now tell me, where do you live?"

"Mostly, on the back side of Lost Mineral Hill. That's the one with the big white 'T' on it. I got a nice tent with a wood floor, wood stove, and all the fixin's. It sets neatly in a small gulch surrounded by a bunch of quakin' aspens. Jest fine for me. 'Cept for a rattlesnake now and then. They likes my warm wood floor on those cool nights. They got me a couple times. Mostly, I get them dead."

"I understand. What's your address?"

"Ain't got no address. No need for one. Never gits no mail. And nobody visits."

"Interesting. Go to school?"

"Yup. All the way through the third grade. That's when mama died of consumption. And I been on my own ever since. I can read and write mostly, and I can recite the Preamble to the Declaration of Independence. Want to hear it?"

"No, thank you. Nonetheless, I am impressed. You limp and walk with a cane. Care to talk about it?"

"Nothin' to be 'shamed of. I enlisted in '97 when those damnable Spaniards sunk our battleship Main in Havana, Cuba. I was a Rough Rider with Teddy at San Juan Hill. Got a Spanish bullet in my hip—still there. Wanna see my Purple Heart medal? Carry it in my pocket. Teddy hisself pinned it on my blouse."

"I am impressed. I did not realize you are a wounded veteran. Now, Josh, please tell me what happened last Sunday."

"Well, it's simple enough. Melissa and Matilda, twin sisters they are, are two lady friends of mine. And I emphasize 'lady,' 'cause that's jest what they be. And they are sorta friends exactly and no more—'cept me and Mattie and I did some sparking after that evangelist revival meetin' some years back. Nothin' more, mind you. Now, don't get no funny ideas. 'Cause it ain't true."

"I believe you. Please continue."

"After services, Matilda asked me if I'd want to go with them to Goldfield. About thirty miles down highway number 95. It's not paved. But the bottom is good and hard and is passable most times. But not when it rains so hard in the winter. There's always washouts that need fixin'."

"I understand. And then what?"

"They was a goin' to the brand new Goldfield Hotel to see one of them motion pictures that talk. It's almost like real people talkin' to you, she said. I wondered how them fellas done make the pictures talk. That's somethin' I gotta see."

Goldfield Hotel, Goldfield, Nevada

"Indeed. What happened next?"

"It were last year, I reckon, some fella came to town and rigged up his moving picture machine in the Mustang Saloon. We seen the moving picture show called The It Girl. Ain't no sound with the movin' pictures. But Melissa played music on the player piano. Not roll music, but music where her fingers hit the keys. Right pretty girl in the pictures, Clara Bow or somebody. A wonderful evening. I sure like that actress. She so pretty and spry."

Clara Bow

"Please get on with your story, Josh. We don't have lots of time."

"If you say so. I forgot to tell ya that them two women were dressed to the nines. Those flapper dresses was too short for their age. And, of course, they had a pair of matching parasols. I was in my usual blue denim coveralls, calf-length, lace-up boots, need 'em in the outback. I don't cotton to them city-type clothes."

"Josh, I don't need those details. The essence, please!"

Ford Model T (Flivver)

"Well, the women got into their flivver to drive down to Goldfield. Matilda was in the driver's position. I cranked the flivver to get it started. But, damn it, Matilda kept messing up setting the spark jest right. The flivver wouldn't start, and my right arm was beginning to hurt somethin' awful. Do you know how much effort one has to use to crank a flivver?"

"No! And I don't care. Sorry. Then what happened?"

"Then I has to do it. I reckon Matilda fiddled with the spark on purpose so's I'd have to sit on her lap to work that spark lever. I set it correctly and told her to keep her hands off it. I got out, twirled the crank just once, and that engine began to purr. I got the flivver started. Them two women is tricky. Arranged the seating so as I had to sit right between them. Anyway, we got moving down highway number 91 to Goldfield."

"I see that it is it ten minutes to the hour. What happened next?"

"Those two biddies started yammering 'bout this and that of no point that I could see. Those high-pitched voices never stopped blabbering. Screeching it was. Once, I tried to ask them to be quiet and enjoy the scenery. But them chatterboxes never stopped jabbering. And, I got tell you, thet continuous, high-pitch noise was irritating my soul no end. I jammed my hands over my ears to shut out the blabber. Didn't work. That screeching was a buzz saw cuttin' up my brain."

"I can understand your feelings."

"Feelings, my ass. I was goin' out of my head. When would they ever stop? Eventually, we entered Goldfield. Now Goldfield ain't the biggest town in Nevada, but it is the county seat of Esmeralda County. Last year I found out 'bout Esmeralda. You know who she was?"

"Of course."

"Well, tell me. I want to see if you're so damn smart after all."

"No! Continue. We have to complete our chat."

"I'll give you a hint. She was a French woman."

"I don't know, and I don't give a damn. We have to complete this interview, now."

"To continue, Esmeralda has got a hardware store with all sorts of mining equipment, a dozen saloons, two dry goods emporiums, three barber shops, lots of eateries, that brand new hotel, and four bordellos. I otta' know."

"I beg you, Josh, we are almost out of time. We have to get to the end of your story. Is that crystal clear?"

"I reckon it's clear, but I don't know what's the hurry. You goin' someplace?"

"Indeed, I am. And so are you. Get on with it."

"To continue. My brain was buzzing with this intense pain and I didn't know what to do. We were driving the main street and out of nowhere, Melissa yells, 'Stop!' She had spotted a dress, or a hat, or shoes, or somethin' in the display window of one of them emporiums. She and Matilda bolted into the store. I sat there ready to scream. Time was a wastin'. Sometime later these women return to the flivver, arms loaded with boxes wrapped with fancy ribbons and bows. They tossed that loot into the back. Matilda told me to wait. They had more shopping to do. And that's what they did, shop, jammer, shop, blabber, shop, and yammer. The pain was driving me out of my mind."

"Do you believe that you were crazy?"

"No. I was crazy with them two women making my life miserable. Well, anyway, finally they returned to the flivver, dumped in lots more shopping stuff, got in, and we got started to the hotel just a ways down the main street. We got there shortly. Guess what we seen?"

"I couldn't imagine. Why don't you tell me?"

"The folks were coming out of the hotel: smiling, chatting, shaking hands, and all thet. The movin' picture show was over. Those two damn twin women made me miss seeing a real live talking picture. Such a calamity was more than my soul could bear. I couldn't stand it no more."

"And?"

"The rest is kinda fuzzy. But I knowed that I couldn't take it no more. I drew my six gun and put three bullets dead center into the chest of each one of them twins. I done it, all right. But I didn't mean to. I don't remember the rest of it."

"Josh, looks as if they are waiting for us. Let's go. Perhaps the judge won't hang you."

USS SAN ANTONIO

Captain Rafael Hubner, skipper of the *USS San Antonio*, the Navy's newest dirigible, shouted, "Cast off the forward lines."

The Chief Boatswain snapped, "Aye, Aye Sir." In a second, the airship's bow dipped upward slightly.

"Cast off the aft lines."

"Aft lines, Aye."

"Engineman, one-quarter power."

"Aye, Sir. One-quarter power."

The eight Maybach engines sent a throbbing vibration throughout the leviathan as it inched forward and the *USS San Antonio* gently gained altitude. The Naval Air Station at Moffett, California faded slowly into the background.

USN, ZRS-6 San Antonio

"Helmsman, two degrees starboard."

"Two degrees starboard. Aye, Sir."

"Steady as she goes."

"Steady, Aye."

"Release five-hundred pounds ballast fore and aft."

"Five-hundred pounds Aye, Sir."

Streams of water fell from the dirigible and it leaped into the air.

"Three-quarters power."

"Aye, Sir, three-quarters power."

The Maybach engines roared to life and the four-bladed propellers spun at blinding speed. The *USS San Antonio* accelerated to its cruising speed of eighty-five knots and leveled off at six-thousand feet. All's well as the ship began its maiden cross-country flight to participate in the Fifth Fleet's annual exercises off the east coast.

"Mister Able, plot a course to Yuma via San Diego."

"Yuma, Sir," replied the navigator.

The skipper was taking the southern route to cross the country where the ground elevations are the lowest. The *San Antonio* dirigible does not have the lifting power to sail over the Rocky Mountains.

"Chief Aerographer, what's the wind direction and velocity?'

"Sir, last reading, four minutes ago, the wind was seven knots at zero, two, zero degrees true. Indications are an increasing velocity over the next few hours." He fiddles with his instruments and charts. Barometer reading on the ground is 29.0 inches of mercury. "Looks as if a small system is developing over northern Colorado.

"Very well. Keep me posted."

The farms in San Joaquin Valley unfold as the dirigible heads south."

"Status report navigator,"

"On course." He pauses to check his charts. "That north tail wind has increased and has boosted our ground speed to ninety-seven knots."

A small frown crossed Captain Hubner's brow. "Chief Shaw, what's the status?"

"Sir, north wind at twelve knots,"

"Your prediction, Chief."

"Captain, I need a few minutes to take readings and plot the results.'

"Very well."

The *San Antonio* sailed over the city of Los Angeles. Some of the crew stared at the colossus and wondered how its denizens lived in that sprawl, and where did Clara Bow live and were the stories about her and the University of Southern California football team true.

"Radioman Chung, send a status report message to Operations at Moffett."

"Status report, Aye. Aye, Sir."

Chief Shaw, the aerographer, reported, "Captain, the wind is increasing. It's now fifteen knots. That system over Colorado has expanded rapidly due to high-level winds barreling down from Canada."

"Forecast?"

"Hard to tell, Sir. The system is building rapidly. It may fizzle out over the desert in Arizona and New Mexico, or it could pick up energy from the radiated heat and increase significantly. I'm getting reports of scattered showers in Flagstaff and Grants."

Over San Diego, Captain Hubner ordered, "Navigator, set our course for Yuma."

"To compensate for the crosswind, I recommend zero, eight, zero."

"Very well, Helmsman, steer zero, eight, zero."

"Zero, eight, zero, Aye. Sir.

The *San Antonio* gradually swung to the east, and glided over the California desert. The rising heat expanded the Helium in the ship's gas bags and the airship began to rise—slowly at first then more rapidly passing eight-thousand feet.

"Helmsman, elevator down five degrees."

"Five degrees down. Aye."

"Boatswain, release seven-thousand cubic meters of Helium."

"Seven thousand, yes sir."

The ship now less buoyant and with its nose pointed slightly downward, stopped its rise, and the crew returned it to its cruising altitude of six-thousand feet.

"Up elevator five degrees."

"Five degrees, Sir."

The navigator said, "Passing over Yuma in two minutes."

"Set a course for El Paso."

Without asking the aerographer announced, "Captain, the north wind is now twenty-one knots and the barometric pressure is 28.5 and dropping."

"Very well. Keep me posted."

"Will do."

The navigator completed his calculations, "Recommend heading of zero, nine, zero."

An hour later, the *San Antonio*, on its new heading passed, over Gila Bend. With the strong crosswind, the skipper ordered the helmsman more rudder corrections.

"Captain, we're over Tucson and its elevation is 2,400 feet. Now our true altitude is only 3,600 feet."

"Thanks, Chief. We need a couple thousand feet." Hubner checked the instrument panel and the navigator charts. "Boatswain, release two-thousand pounds ballast."

"Two-thousand. Aye, Sir."

The water dropped from the forward and aft tanks and a few homes in Tucson had their lawns watered at no charge. The airship sailed over Deming whose elevation is 4,300 feet. The ship's barometric altitude instrument indicated that it was at sixty-five hundred feet. But because of the rising ground elevation it was only at twenty-three hundred feet over the town. The outside thermometer indicated the air temperature had dropped and now was forty-two degrees Fahrenheit.

"Captain!" shouted the chief aerographer. "Thunderheads are forming on a line South of Santa Fe and Albuquerque and moving south and moving rapidly." He checked another instrument, "Wind velocity is thirty-five knots and increasing."

Captain Hubner immediately ordered the helmsman to steer another seven-degrees starboard to offset that strong crosswind and to keep the *San Antonio* close to its proposed course.

"Realizing the perilous danger ahead, Hubner went to the navigator's chart table, studied the maps, and asked Lieutenant Able, "Should we turn around and head west to more friendly weather?"

"Not feasible, Sir. That north wind would shove us deep into Mexico and this storm will follow us." He used his instruments to plot a direct course to El Paso. Our best option is to race for Fort Bliss in El Paso. Elevation is 3,800 feet, and we might be able to dock there and ride out this storm."

"Agreed." Captain Hubner ordered the engineman, "Full speed ahead."

Lieutenant Mark LeShack, the Operations Office at Naval Air Station Moffett, tapped his fingers on his desk and spoke to the radioman, "Its been over an hour ago since we received a situation report from the *San Antonio*." He rose and went to the aerographer's desk, studied the current weather charts, and said, "That fast-moving system has developed into a full-fledged, high-energy thunderstorm. "Radioman, try again to raise the *San Antonio*."

"Yes sir." He twisted dials and spoke into his microphone, "NAS Moffett calling *USS San Antonio*. Over." After several seconds, "No response, Sir."

"Keep trying."

"Yes, Sir." After a dozen broadcasts, he said, "No response."

"Try long-wave communications."

The radioman, expertly tapped his Morse-code key sending a string of dots and dashes. He waited 60 seconds and did not receive a response. He tried again. Again. Again. And again. All in vain. The *USS San Antonio* did not respond.

PRINCE FEODOR

Peking

August 1936

Prince Feodor Alexandrovich Romanov walks across Tiananmen Square. His light-grey suit, tailored by a former Moscow couturier, is respectable but slightly rumpled. It is far from the expensive and expertly tailored clothes he wore at the court of his uncle—Czar Nicholas II.

Feodor is now thirty-eight years old, but his manner is that of a man much older. His pace is slower and his stride is shorter. His hair is thinner and laced with streaks of white. His once handsome face reflects the horror of the Bolshevik Revolution and the years of sorrow he's suffered at the murder of his beloved wife and two darling children at the hands of the Cheka, the Soviet secret police. He hardly notices the throng of people zigzagging every which way throughout the square. He focuses on his delicate mission in this strange city.

His years as an expatriate living with a small cadre of White Russians in Peking have eroded his royal mien. Yet there is still about Feodor the shadow of a more sophisticated and affluent past.

Occasionally, his mind wanders to his longing for a better life. It lies with Magdalena, a former member of the White Russian cadre with whom he's had a brief affair that kindled their deep affection. She is a widow whose husband, Colonel Rostislav Makarenko, fought with the White Army of Admiral Kolchak and was killed by shrapnel from an exploding Red artillery shell near Kazan.

Feodor reflects on how he met Magdalena. It had been only the year before, at a White Russian party celebrating the anniversary of the ascension of Nicholas Romanov as Czar of all the Russias. The venue was Oretsky's Russian Teahouse—a gathering place for the Whites in Peking. The Russian musicians' repertoire extended beyond the traditional folk songs to some graceful waltzes, and soon the audience had pushed tables aside to create a small dance floor. The vodka flowed freely, and happy laughter and joyful music filled the room. Feodor had settled in to enjoy the music and, for the first time in many months, he was at ease and content.

"I wonder if I may join you?" A tall, slender woman stood beside his table. "There are no other places available."

Magdalena

"Yes, of course." He rose and pulled out a chair.

The woman was somewhat older than he, attractive and well groomed. She sat gracefully and smiled amicably. "Thank you." Up close, Feodor saw that her face showed lines of weariness, and she wore a little too much makeup in a marginally successful effort to conceal her low spirits.

She wore a silk gown in the style of the previous decade, of fine quality but slightly faded. On her ears were heavy pearl earrings, and her thick blonde hair was carefully dressed.

She spoke softly as the orchestra paused between tunes. "May I introduce myself?" Hers was the voice of a well-educated, upper-class Russian.

"Yes, please."

"I am Countess Magdalena Ulanova Makarenko, formerly of Novgorod." She paused to correct her statement and her smile was faint but warm. "No longer a Countess, but now a seamstress eking out a paltry living in a millinery shop. And you?"

"I'm Feodor Alexandrovich Romanov, formerly of Saint Petersburg, trying to find purpose in my life and a way to earn a living. Unfortunately, I have no marketable skills."

Magdalena recognized the name and gasped in surprise. "The nephew of the Czar? The Prince Feodor?"

"No longer a prince, my lady. But just another displaced White Russian with meager means and realizing with all my soul that the Russia we knew is gone and can never be again." Feodor noticed her faint perfume. "May I offer you a vodka? I'm about to order another."

She smiled again and nodded. "Yes, that would be nice. Thank you."

They sat and chatted pleasantly for a time. Her well-mannered reserve appealed to Feodor. When the orchestra played a Tchaikovsky waltz, he invited her to dance. She was as graceful on her feet as he—they were a beautiful couple. Without a word, they danced the next three waltzes as if they were at a court ball. The orchestra paused for a few moments as the musicians shuffled their sheet music. Much to the surprise of all, the orchestra next played Hoagy Carmichael's love song Star Dust, and mimicked Artie Shaw's orchestration. The big-band music from America filled the teahouse with hope and romance. Magdalena snuggled next to Feodor and placed her head on his shoulder as they glided through the sensuous foxtrot, a faint hint of passion aroused in both dancers.

Somewhat awkwardly, they returned to their table. Magdalena looked off into the distance. For a moment she was silent, her thoughts apparently elsewhere. She tossed down the last of her vodka and rose to leave. "It's late, and I must go." With her biggest smile she said, "Thank you, Feodor, for your courtesy and this delightfully entertaining evening."

Feodor rose quickly. "Would you allow me to escort you home? The streets may not be safe for a woman alone at this time of night."

She nodded slowly with a faint smile. "Of course."

Feodor paid his bill and escorted Magdalena outside, where he hailed a rickshaw. Speaking in Mandarin, she gave the driver an address, and they set off into the dark streets. They rode silently for a few minutes. Feodor noticed her shivering under her thin shawl; he pulled off his jacket and draped it over her shoulders.

"Thank you," she murmured.

After a few minutes, Feodor spoke softly, somewhat embarrassed. "Perhaps you know of a place where I might pawn a few items to tide me over for a few weeks?"

Magdalena smiled inwardly as she realized that Prince Feodor was just as destitute as almost all the White Russians in China. She knew that most survived by selling their jewelry. She responded, "When I need something extra, there's always the Wuhan's Antiks shop. He's unscrupulous, of course, but he pays better than the other dealers for first-rate pieces and does not ask questions." Feodor stored this critical information away—shortly he would visit Wuhan's Antiks.

"We have arrived." She pointed to a small, Western-style millinery shop. "I have a room above the shop."

Feodor helped her down from the rickshaw and escorted her to the door. "Thank you for a pleasant evening," he said as she gave him her hand. He bowed to kiss it. "Goodnight."

Magdalena asked if he would like to come in for a vodka nightcap. He nodded and dismissed the rickshaw. He followed her through a door next to the shop, up a narrow staircase, and into her room. Her lodging was small and simple—a round, Chinese-style table and a few chairs, a settee covered with a faded silk brocade, a tiny stove, and a large Coromandel screen, behind which he could see the foot of a bed. The worn floor was covered with a once fine Chinese rug. On the wall was an icon set in a chased silver-gilt frame. The room smelled faintly of Magdalena's perfume.

"Please take the settee." She withdrew a bottle of vodka and a pair of glasses from a cupboard. "I have no caviar, I'm sorry to say, but these Chinese biscuits go rather well with vodka." Feodor detected her nervousness as she bustled around preparing their drinks.

She poured the vodka, and they toasted each other, and to better days and more civilized times. They chatted about their lost Russia, Lenin's regicide of the Czar and his family, and the impoverished White Russians trying to survive in this Oriental city. And, the vodka flowed freely. The libations eased her reserve and she mentioned that her first cousin had emigrated to Vancouver several years before in hope of a new life in a Western country. Several months earlier, she said, she'd applied for a visa at the Canadian Embassy to join her cousin.

"Are you as thrilled as I, Feodor?"

"Indeed, I am." Inside his heart, however, the pangs of distress stabbed his soul. His newfound friend would soon be leaving. Here was a woman he could grow to love.

The conversation sagged, and Magdalena looked at her hands, then around the room. Wandering nervously, she straightened a flower in the vase on her table, and then replenished the biscuits on the plate.

Finally, Magdalena took a deep breath and sat on the settee next to Feodor. Taking both his hands in hers, she spoke. "You're a fine man, Feodor. I appreciate that you have treated me with respect this evening." She placed the fingers of her right hand on his cheek and gently stroked it. She stopped for a moment, blushing deeply. Then she slipped her right arm around his neck, then her left arm, and gently pulled him close to her. She kissed him passionately, and in a soft, stumbling voice whispered, "Make love to me tonight."

Over the next several days, Feodor met Magdalena every evening at Oretsky's, and they settled into a pattern of eating the evening meal together and talking long into the night. Feodor found comfort in her refined manner, and he relished their long conversations, which ranged from literature to world events. He was strongly attracted to her elegant body and unbridled lovemaking. At closing time, they retreated to her apartment to satiate their passion.

One evening Magdalena arrived at Oretsky's with a broad smile on her face. She rushed to Feodor's table and with intense joy in her voice, almost shouted, "My visa papers arrived today at the Canadian embassy. At last I'll be free!" She twirled to express her happiness and her skirt flared. "I leave tomorrow. I'm taking the express train to Shanghai, and then in three days I'll board the Pacific and Orient steamship S.S. Cathay bound for Vancouver." Then, in a most unladylike way she shouted, "Hooray for Canada!"

Feodor felt a serious inner conflict: delight that Magdalena soon would be moving to a new and better life, but distress that he would lose her. He mastered his deep emotions and gave her hand a warm squeeze. "I'm glad for you." Ignoring protocol, he wrapped his arms around her and kissed her fully on the mouth. No longer could he control his emotions. With a sob catching in his throat, he murmured, "My God, I'll miss you, my darling."

"Don't say it. Please don't say it. Let my happiness pervade this our final evening. Know this, my dear Feodor, one day I could love you with all my heart and passion, but not now." Several small tears fell from her eyes. "You know my heart."

"I understand."

As they ate dinner, Magdalena chatted happily about her plans for her life in Canada. Frustration weighed heavily on Feodor. He dreaded the moment of Magdalena's impending departure. He'd be alone again, bereft of both friendship and their comfortable passion. Nonetheless, he maintained a joyous manner.

Then, as had become their custom, Feodor escorted Magdalena to her lodging. Their lovemaking was tender with sadness and resignation. Feodor wondered whether, in another time and place, their relationship might have blossomed into something more enduring.

As he dressed to leave, Magdalena spoke. "I have a keepsake I want you to have." She opened her hand to reveal a heavy gold medal of St. Andrew on a thick gold chain. "This belonged to my husband and has been in his family for generations. It's very dear to me." She slipped the chain over his head. "At our parting now, I want you to have it. Perhaps it will protect you and bring you comfort in your future." She hugged and kissed Feodor and tears dropped on her cheek. "You will always be in my heart and in my prayers."

Feodor returned her kiss. "As you will be in mine."

Magdalena's slow, soft smile shone on him. "Yes, my dear Feodor. My heart breaks to leave you." She released her embrace. "There are always so many things left to say, but let's not say them. I know what you have meant to me, and I to you. I'll never forget you." She handed him a slip of paper. "My address in Vancouver. Please write to me from time to time."

"Of course, my dear Magdalena." Feodor paused at the door, turned, and said, "Go with God, my dear friend."

With trepidation, Feodor turned into Tsingtao Street a few blocks south of Tiananmen Square. The dark, narrow passage was more an alley than a street. Overhead, placards stretched across the alley between the multistory buildings and nearly obscured the late afternoon sunshine. The alley was lined with a menagerie of establishments that offered a sundry variety of wares for sale or barter: herbs from gentle palliatives to deadly poisons, antiques and knickknacks, jewelry from junk to priceless gems. Apothecaries offered drugs from aspirin to laudanum. A live animal shop sold everything from hares to cobras. Other vendors hawked vegetables, butchered meat, French pastries, apparel from workers' garments to haute-couture ensembles, pipes of opium, and women of easy virtue.

Several blocks down the alley, Feodor spotted his objective: Wuhan's Antiks. The sign over the door read simply "Antiks." As Feodor entered, a small bell attached to the door tinkled softly. The shop was jammed with bric-a-brac and tourist souvenirs, with barely enough room for anyone to move about. These items belied the true nature of this place. The proprietor, Wuhan Wei-kuo, emerged from behind a black, beaded curtain at the back of the shop. He was of indeterminate age and short of stature. This day he was dressed in a black gown, and a skull cap with a long red tassel covered his short black hair. His penetrating black eyes dominated his lean, expressionless face. With his alert manner, he projected the air of a no-nonsense businessman.

Wuhan was the premier dealer of valuable antiques in Peking. For steep fees, he represented foreigners at auctions and in clandestine private sales of valuable Oriental antiques. Lacking scruples and having superior knowledge of antiques, archeological artifacts, and the black market for such items, he negotiated all deals to his own pecuniary advantage. He was not above skirting the legalities of the Antiquities Department in order to foster a lucrative deal.

Feodor greeted Wuhan in Russian. Wuhan bowed in greeting, turned to part the beaded curtain behind him, and spoke in Mandarin in a low voice to his niece, Yen Hei-lan, who was in the office in the back.

Yen Hei-lan glided into the customer area of the shop and greeted Feodor in fluent Russian. "My uncle and I welcome you, sir, to our humble establishment." She wore a red, skintight cheongsam, slit to the upper thigh. A golden dragon embroidered on the cheongsam wrapped its way sinuously around her bewitching body. Hei-lan was a startlingly beautiful, sexy woman with long shapely legs and large, almond eyes that sparkled with wicked sin. She had a wide, full-lipped mouth, high cheekbones, glowing pale-olive skin, and long black hair cascading over her shoulders. Her wasp-thin waist enhanced her near-perfect figure. As she spoke, she looked boldly at Feodor with a provocative smile.

Feodor stared at her, awestruck by her exotic beauty and her coquettish mien. Somewhat awkwardly, he nodded and gave a short bow. Trying to recoup his composure he muttered, "Thank you, Miss. I am Feodor Alexandrovich. "

Hei-lan responded with a small bow and expanded her smile. "We are much pleased that you have come to visit us—possibly to do some small business? Perhaps we can be of service." Notwithstanding Feodor's outward countenance, she took the measure of him as a man of faded savoir-faire, someone who once enjoyed a degree of importance and still commanded respect. She purred, "You have come far, I suspect. Please sit at our table and let me offer you a cup of tea to relieve your fatigue. It is more pleasant to do business when one is comfortable." Beneath her calm exterior, Hei-lan experienced a shiver of curiosity and excitement. Her incredibly sharp memory flashed, and she knew immediately that this fellow indeed was Prince Feodor Alexandrovich Romanov—nephew of the late Czar Nicholas II. Intrigued, she speculated that this Romanov prince was just another desperate White Russian down on his luck.

She escorted Feodor to a softly-lit lounge behind the jumbled shop. She had furnished it with soft leather chairs, a large teak and ebony coffee table, and thick silk carpets. An étagère held a collection of exquisite Sung celadons, and a magnificent brush painting of a karst mountain landscape hung on the paneled wall. As Hei-lan moved to the table, the clinging cheongsam enhanced her every curve. Her provocative movements intensified Feodor's discomfort. He slid uneasily into a high-backed chair covered with bright green silk.

The diminutive Wuhan took an adjoining chair. Hei-lan sat across from Feodor, focusing on his eyes. "My name is Yen Hei-lan, but please call me Black Orchid. That is what my name means in your language." A faint hint of her exotic perfume suffused throughout the room.

On Wuhan's subtle signal, a young female servant brought tea and cakes. Wuhan dismissed her sharply after she stared ever so briefly at Feodor. Black Orchid poured tea for the three of them and passed the cakes. After a polite pause and a sip or two, Black Orchid asked coaxingly, "How may we be of service?"

Feodor cleared his throat. "I'm not quite sure how to begin. I'm here on delicate business that requires scrupulous discretion."

In her most soothing voice Black Orchid said, "We understand. We are experienced in such circumstances. Please be relaxed and tell us about this delicate business. We will listen carefully and do what we can to be of assistance."

Feodor, somewhat reassured, said, "Friends have recommended Wuhan's Antiks for a fair deal."

She smiled. "We are honored to enjoy that reputation. Please, do continue."

Not sure how to proceed in this alien environment, Feodor replied in a soft, tentative voice, almost a whisper, "I have a necklace for sale. A rare, jeweled necklace." As he spoke, he gained more confidence and his words more authority. "The owner is an old friend who wants to remain anonymous. This person needs funds and has asked me to act as his intermediary," he lied.

"Indeed, you have intrigued us. Do you have this necklace with you?"

"Yes, I have it."

"Excellent. Perhaps it would be best to let us inspect it."

Feodor withdrew a chamois pouch from his coat's inner pocket and removed a heavy emerald-and-diamond necklace. He handed it to Black Orchid.

"Thank you, Mister Alexandrovich," she said with a large smile and fluttering eyelashes. "This necklace is indeed beautiful. My uncle is the expert with such items." She carefully handed the necklace to Wuhan.

Wuhan drew a jeweler's loupe from an inner pocket of his black gown. Under the loupe's ten-power magnification, he carefully inspected the magnificent piece. He spotted the Romanovs' double-eagle royal crest engraved on the back of the catch. On reflection, he was convinced that this necklace was part of the missing Romanov collection from the Soviet Union. As he examined each gem and the intricate platinum setting, he wondered if the necklace was a solo item, or came from a cache of the other missing jewelry. There were no clues as to how the Romanov family jewels had vanished, where they were, or who was responsible for their disappearance. Wuhan was intrigued. He mused to himself, How does this shabby Russian come to have this rare royal treasure? Who is his patron who owns this necklace? And why is this treasure for sale?

Wuhan turned to Feodor. Speaking through Black Orchid as Russian interpreter, he said, "May I ask how your 'old friend' came to have this necklace in his possession? It appears to be from the missing Romanov collection."

Cautiously, Feodor responded, "That is a matter I am not privileged to discuss."

"Very well," Wuhan responded, with a hint of disappointment in his eyes. He turned and whispered instructions to Black Orchid in Mandarin.

Black Orchid flashed a smile and said, "May I ask what you are asking for this necklace? And, should we conclude a propitious bargain, in what currency would you prefer payment? Or would you prefer gold, valued in United States dollars at yesterday's closing price on the Chicago Board of Trade?"

"No, I do not want to deal in gold, and I do not want American dollars, which are too weak on the international market. The American Depression has severely devalued the dollar." After brief reflection, Feodor said, "I would prefer payment in British pounds sterling. I understand that this is the only currency that is stable and has worldwide acceptance. Do you approve?"

"Of course," she responds. "And your price?"

Feodor stumbled. Unfortunately, he had no concept of the necklace's worth and realized that he had made a fool of himself by not doing comprehensive research. He did know that it had to be very expensive. Hesitantly, he responded, "Seventy five thousand pounds—a most reasonable price for this rare and valuable necklace from the house of Romanov."

"Thank you, Mister Alexandrovich." She glanced at Wuhan for his signal, then nodded with understanding. "Please know that, because of the notoriety surrounding this necklace that once belonged to the Romanov royal family, we must be absolutely discreet if we purchase it. Should the Soviet government discover our involvement, we would become prime targets for justice from the Cheka."

"Be assured that only my principal and I know of my visit. We have no desire for this transaction to be made public."

Black Orchid nodded and looked for a signal from her uncle. She made a counteroffer of thirty-five-thousand pounds. Feodor refused with a negative headshake. They continued dickering for the next several minutes without agreement. Black Orchid rose to pour more tea, and she made sure that her cheongsam worked its erotic charm. Through sips of tea, Black Orchid relayed Wuhan's offers and Feodor's counteroffers. Eventually, they agreed on fifty-five-thousand pounds.

Wuhan showed no emotion. However, inwardly he was exceedingly pleased with this surprisingly lucrative bargain. He knew that this Romanov necklace would fetch upwards of £200,000, perhaps much more, from the black-market collectors with whom he dealt.

Black Orchid purred, "Congratulations, Mister Alexandrovich. You have bargained astutely. Let us conclude this business. To what name shall we make our check payable?"

Feodor responded somewhat sharply, "Miss Yen. I would prefer cash, if you please."

Somewhat taken aback by the sharpness of his response, Black Orchid said, "Please excuse me if I have offended you. Regrettably, it is not possible to pay in cash. We do not keep such funds here in our shop. It would be foolish to invite blackguards to rob us. We will pay by a check written on the China National Bank and Trust Company here in Peking. My uncle will telephone the bank's senior teller, Mister Chan Sen-tao, to confirm that our check will clear with your identification and endorsement." She caught Feodor's eye and in the same even, relaxed way asked, "In what name shall we make our check payable?"

Black Orchid's question caught Feodor off guard. He leaned back in his chair and looked away at a curved ivory tusk in the shop's interior as he carefully formed his reply. "I'm embarrassed to admit that I would be in an awkward predicament trying to cash a check. I have no papers. No passport. No form of identification. I'm in China, as you might say, 'unauthorized.' Legally, I am a nonperson. With the chaos engulfing this country, no one has bothered me, especially since I am an Occidental."

Black Orchid replied with feigned sympathy, "It is as we suspected. Your predicament is familiar to us. Over the past several years, we have dealt with many White Russians in similar circumstances. All with mutual satisfaction, I might add."

Feodor said, "If you can make satisfactory arrangements, then please make the check payable to Bearer."

Black Orchid countered in a smooth, indifferent voice, "That is not possible. We cannot write our check as you ask. That would be careless business, especially for this amount of money. We would be courting danger for you and for us in these troubled times. Besides, Mister Chan will demand identification and a signature."

"Are we then at an impasse?" asked Feodor dejectedly.

"Not at all. Perhaps there is a way. We have dealt with an associate who might be of service. He can produce an authentic-looking passport with appropriate visas for you that will satisfy the closest inspection. If this opportunity is satisfactory, tell us of what country you want to be a citizen. And what name will you use?"

Intrigued by Black Orchid's offer, Feodor replied, "What is this man's fee for such a service?" He stumbled for a moment in embarrassment. "At the moment, I am short of funds."

"His fee is nominal, and we will cover it. This is part of our service for our treasured clients."

Feodor responded quickly, "Because of my accent and upbringing, I suspect that the country ought to be a Slavic nation. Can that associate of yours make a Polish passport?"

She smiled. "Yes, of course. Any country is possible."

"Use the name Zinovy Annikov," answered Feodor. "He was a friend of mine, a former colleague, who died in the Revolution."

"My sympathies for your loss. Please be patient. Such detailed work will take several hours, and our associate will need your photograph. Come with me to the back of our shop and I will take your photograph with our new Graflex camera. In the meantime, my uncle will telephone our associate, Mister Ling Ping-shu, to tell him about your needs." She handed Feodor a business card. "Here is Mister Ling's address. It is three doors down the street. His sign says, "Draftsman." When ready, our shop girl will take your photograph to the draftsman."

While the process of taking and developing Feodor's photograph proceeded, Wuhan wrote the check to 'Zinovy Annikov' on a special account. He telephoned Chan Sen-tao at the China National Bank and Trust Company, and Chan acknowledged that he would honor the check in cash with proper identification and signature.

Feodor and Black Orchid returned to the table and engaged in a desultory conversation. She flirted provocatively as the slit migrate upwardly. The ever-stoic Wuhan handed his check to Feodor, who inspected it and found it in order. He folded it carefully and put it in his jacket pocket. He stood, made a short bow, smiled, and thanked his host and hostess.

Black Orchid responded, "It is our pleasure, I assure you." As Feodor turned to leave, Black Orchid touched his arm and said in a low voice, "In the Middle Kingdom, it is our custom to conclude a successful business transaction with tea to have pleasant feelings."

Wuhan gave a knowing glance to Black Orchid. She knew exactly what to do. She stood in a provocative pose and in her most soothing voice said, "I will prepare the tea for us. We have a rare and very special oolong from Fujian that we reserve for only the most important occasions."

Feodor, his eyes narrowing thoughtfully as he regarded Black Orchid's exotic form, replied, "Yes, please." He returned to his chair and watched her as she exited the office. Her cheongsam-covered derriere swirled in erotic syncopation. His pulse was several beats faster than usual.

In the back of the shop, Black Orchid concocted her special tea. She spiked Feodor's cup with a libido-enhancing herb, and a small drop of hashish to confuse his mind. Returning to the lounge, she served the tea and they toasted each other. Soon they concluded the tea ritual. Feodor was pleased with himself for the propitious bargain he had concluded. He flashed a broad smile and gave a short bow to Black Orchid and Wuhan.

It was twilight as Feodor left the shop and stepped into the alley. He was proud of himself for the way he had outfoxed Wuhan—settling for a price far more than he had imagined. He hailed a rickshaw conveniently positioned just a few feet from the entrance. As he climbed onto the rickshaw, Black Orchid exited Wuhan's shop. Her long stride exposed her left leg provocatively. "Will you give me a lift to my apartment? It is close by," she purred.

Somewhat euphoric from the drugged tea and dazzled by her sensuous beauty, Feodor nodded agreement. "It is my pleasure."

Black Orchid's penthouse overlooked the Forbidden City. She had furnished it with fine art-deco pieces. Hanging on the walls was an array of paintings by Impressionist masters—Cézanne, Monet, Van Gogh. She also had several pieces by Piet Mondrian—excellent forgeries of which hung in various museums and private collections around the world.

In the early morning, wearing a filmy black negligee, Black Orchid searched Feodor's jacket pockets as he slept off a frenzied night of wild sex, hashish, and Dom Perignon Reserve 1919. She slipped her uncle's check from his jacket.

She wondered if Feodor knew the location of the rest of the missing pieces of the Romanov jewelry. She realized that here was a propitious opportunity for enormous profit and astounding power.

Smiling pleasantly to herself, Black Orchid opened her negligee and gazed at her image in the mirror of a fine, shagreen-covered, French Art Deco vanity. Admiring her sensuous body, she shivered slightly, evoking the exquisite erotic pleasures she had luxuriated in the evening before. A smirk crept over her face as she recalled what the nuns at St. Elizabeth's Academy for Young Ladies had taught her about the virtues of chastity. She speculated on the horror Sister Mary Beatrice O'Hara would have experienced had she witnessed her seduction of Feodor and her delicious enjoyment of their carnal gratification. Perhaps in the future, she thought, *I'll record my seductions on motion-picture film.*

Ever so slowly, she turned around to change her image in the mirror. With brazen affirmation she uttered, "I am a whore, an especially beautiful and skillful whore—a whore who enjoys her work. And I am proud of it."

Her life had not always been so. Several years earlier, in Kansu Province, Hei-lan's parents had been killed in the crossfire of a battle between the troops of the warlord Marshal Chang Hsueh-liang and Colonel Chiang Kai-shek's Nationalist soldiers. Colonel Chiang had just launched his Northwest Campaign to rout out warlordism in China. Now, Hei-lan was the ward of her uncle, Wuhan Wei-kuo.

With searing pain, she remembered how her uncle had first brought her to his bed. She had been a terrified ten-year-old, bewildered at what he was doing to her, and then overcome by excruciating agony as he stole her virginity. The rapes continued until she was fourteen and pregnant. A torturous abortion by a maladroit midwife was her reward for all those years of subjection and humiliation. Now barren, she relished the fact that nowadays there was no limit to her sexual activity.

Wuhan had then demanded that Black Orchid use her exquisite beauty and exceptional erotic skills to induce his clients to enter into profitable deals. He took his pleasure from a variety of housemaids. After a time, Hei-lan had begun to derive intense sexual pleasure from those trysts. Unknown to her uncle, she had enhanced her personal wealth by accepting valuable gifts from her 'guests.' She had learned that Wuhan easily accepted most of her lies, or else he cared less about losing small treasures when his attention was focused on larger gains.

"Yes, I am a whore," she congratulated herself. And she concluded that if her deductions regarding the Romanov jewels were correct, she would be a fabulously wealthy whore, and free from her heinous uncle. *I can be whomever I choose—Catherine the Great reincarnated, the Queen of Sheba personified, or perhaps an international adventuress with many influential men sniffing for my favors.* She sighed with the satisfaction of the completely surfeited.

Black Orchid turned toward Feodor, lying naked on the bed in a drug-induced stupor. *Now I shall learn precisely where those Romanov jewels are.* She smiled to herself.

Quickly, with thin leather straps, Black Orchid bound the naked Feodor's hands and feet spread-eagle to the bedposts, and then straddled him at the waist. She roused him from his deep sleep with several moderately-hard face slaps. Pinned to the bed and not fully conscious, he mumbled incoherently.

With a stern voice Black Orchid demanded, "Listen to me carefully, Prince Feodor Alexandrovich Romanov. I know exactly who you are and if you do not answer all my questions correctly, I will jam this syringe full of belladonna into your eye and you will die in the agony of the damned."

He thrashed about, testing his binding.

Black Orchid waited patiently for him to settle down. "Tell me truly what I will ask. I have all day to play with you."

Trapped, Feodor, summoning what resolve he had left, spouted, "You harlot, I damn you!"

"What strong words you have for a libertine," Black Orchid snapped mockingly. "Now, let's begin. Yesterday you sold my uncle a fabulous Romanov necklace. Tell me, where are the other pieces of the missing Romanov jewelry?"

He tried to focus his eyes on her. Slurring his words, he responded carefully, "I have no idea where they are. I was never privy to that cache."

"Feodor, you take me for a fool. A child could see through your dishonesty. Enough!" She jammed the syringe deep into his cheek.

He emitted strange guttural sounds as the pain overwhelmed his being. He thrashed violently—anything to ease the agony. The leather straps held tight and cut deep into his ankles and wrists, and his oozing blood stained the sheets. He shrieked barbarically and fell into semi consciousness.

Black Orchid coldly assessed Feodor. After a few minutes, he calmed somewhat. She squeezed an ammonia vial under his nose.

Feodor coughed and coughed and coughed. His eyes opened weakly.

Black Orchid smiled mischievously. "Welcome back to my party, Feodor." She shifted her position so that her face was close to his. After a few seconds, she said coyly, "Look here, Feodor. I have another syringe. This one is filled with morphine." She stuck the needle into his arm and squeezed a few drops of the opiate into him. There was not enough of the palliative to ease his intense, lingering pain.

In a soft, friendly voice she said, "Answer my questions truthfully and I'll give you enough of this narcotic to ease your suffering and send you to paradise." She let Feodor consider her proposition. "If your answers are honest, I'll let you go." She waited a few seconds for his response.

Feodor coughed several times, and a dim light returned to his eyes. Not fully awake, he shook his head negatively. "I do not know," he whispered.

"Feodor, enough of your dissembling. Tell me, where are the remaining pieces of the missing Romanov jewelry? How many pieces are there? What type are they?" The dripping needle was dangerously close to Feodor's cheek.

Feodor muttered, "I don't know."

"Fool!" She pricked his other cheek with the needle. Fiery pain exploded in his face, and he screamed in agony. She waited patiently as Feodor thrashed and screeched. After a time, he calmed. With venom in her voice, she demanded, "Tell me true, or else I will jam this syringe full of belladonna into your eye."

With his hands tied, Feodor could not rub his face to ease the pain. In a few minutes, he sputtered, "I had only that necklace. I know nothing of the rest."

"What!" She glared at him. "You're lying to me, Feodor. Do you believe that I am stupid?" She put the needle on the skin just under his right eye.

Feodor felt its sharp point.

With intensity, she snapped, "Continue with this fabrication and I will blind you with belladonna." She moved the needle menacingly. "Tell me correctly!"

He murmured, "I have told you the truth. I only had that one necklace."

Surprised at his faux pas, her black eyes opened wide. "You were the sole owner of that necklace? Are you telling me that there is no old friend that you represent?"

"Yes. It is so."

"Liars are despicable. And you, Feodor, are a despicably stupid liar." She pricked the skin under his left eye, and with deft skill inserted several drops of the noxious poison.

Feodor screamed and screamed at the unbearable pain and his eye quickly swelled shut. He thrashed so severely that he pushed Black Orchid off, and collapsed into a stupor.

Standing by the left side of the bed, she waited several minutes. Then, waving the ammonia vial under his nose, she asked in a syrupy voice, "Feodor, can you hear me?"

He coughed and coughed, but his eyes remain closed.

"Awaken, my dear Feodor. It's playtime again." Another whiff of the ammonia, and another bout of deep coughing roused him to semi consciousness. He was glassy-eyed and quite still. She felt his pulse and found it weak and unsteady. She realized that he might not survive more torture.

Softly this time and with a crooked smile, she purred, "Feodor, tell me now where are the remaining Romanov jewels?"

In a choking voice that was barely audible, he moaned, "I know nothing more."

Black Orchid wondered, Perhaps there might be a thread of truth in his story. With the amount of pain she had inflicted on Feodor, she was convinced that the naïve fellow no longer had the courage or strength to dissemble.

Black Orchid demanded, "How did you own such a priceless jewel from the Romanov collection?" She gently waved the syringe slowly in front of his left eye.

Feodor was nearly paralyzed with searing pain and his mind was clouded with harrowing fear. He responded between coughs and gasps of air. "My aunt, Grand Duchess Xenia, gave it to my late wife, Princess Irina Pavlovna Paley, as a wedding present."

At last, Black Orchid realized that Feodor had responded with veracity, and severe disappointment pervaded her at the lost opportunity for fabulous riches. In sullen anger, she grabbed the gold chain with the Saint Andrew's medal and yanked it off his neck. She twirled it around several times, then let it drop into her outstretched left hand to feel its heft.

"Nice," she said. "This will make a fine addition to my collection. Tell me, Feodor, how did you come by this gold medal and chain?" She mounted him again. "I'll not tolerate lies. Understand?" She put the syringe under his chin.

Semi-dazed by the excruciating pain, Feodor sputtered, "My friend Magdalena gave it to me as a keepsake."

"Who is this Magdalena?" Black Orchid demanded.

"A White Russian formerly in Peking now gone to Canada."

"Were you lovers?"

"Yes!" he gasped. He paused to gain some resolve. "And proudly so." He began to feel some vitality in his body.

Instantly, Black Orchid realized that perhaps a new line of inquiry had appeared. "Did your Magdalena know about the Romanov jewels?"

With his resolve and strength returning, Feodor said, "Absolutely not. She is a widow from Kazan and was as destitute as most all the White Russians in China."

Black Orchid moved the syringe menacingly close to his right eye. "This is correct?" she demanded.

"It is the truth, I swear. Yes. Yes, of course."

Dejectedly, she abandoned this line of questioning as having no import.

Black Orchid had one last item to resolve. She had to get Feodor's endorsement on her uncle's check. Those funds would significantly enhance the balance of her private bank account.

"Feodor, endorse my uncle's check to me and you may go free. And, if you want, you may have that vial of morphine. If you refuse, you'll feel my wrath with the remaining belladonna."

After a short pause, and realizing that he had no option, Feodor said, "Hand me the check, you despicable strumpet."

Black Orchid uttered a small laugh as she untied Feodor's right hand. "If you are so pure of soul, relay our evening of sinful pleasure to your Magdalena. Omit no detail. Will she love you all the more?" She roared in laughter at her cruel joke.

Just as Black Orchid completed untying Feodor's right hand, he rolled to his left, and in a lightning flash and with all the resolve and strength he could muster, his clenched right fist slammed into her right jaw. The powerful blow knocked her to the floor and her head slammed into the sideboard. After a moment she emited a low groan, and blood-colored spittle oozed from her mouth.

Feodor, in pain and with his mind slightly fuzzy, struggled to free himself. Dressing was an ordeal. He fetched the morphine syringe and injected a portion of the opiate into the median cubital vein in his right arm. In a few seconds his lingering pain began to ease. He recovered his Saint Andrew medal and chain from the floor. Then he spotted Wuhan's check at bedside, grabbed it, and stumbled toward the door. As he passed Black Orchid lying flat on her back, he knelt and took her pulse from the carotid artery. It was a little slow but steady.

He saw that her breathing was regular. He rolled back her eyelids and saw that her eyes were centered. She was alive and only superficially hurt.

She would live. He rolled her to her left side so that her spittle would drain to the floor and not go back into her mouth. Suddenly, as inflamed vengeance blotted out his reason, he knelt, thrust his hands to her throat, and started to choke her. He tightened his grip to rid the planet of this succubus. In a few seconds, he released his grip, stood, and rubbed his hands together. His code would not permit him to murder Black Orchid.

Feodor, with a swollen eye and befuddled by the morning's events and the hypnotic effects of the morphine, walked the streets. After about an hour, he had regained some composure and formulated a plan. He walked toward the alley where Wuhan's Antiks was located, and down the narrow passage until he spotted the sign that read "Draftsman." The address was the same as on the business card that Black Orchid had given him. Assuming that this was the forger's shop, he entered and spotted an elderly gentleman hunched over a large drafting table, working with a T-square, triangles, and drawing pen. Toward the rear of the shop stood a huge roll top desk made of fine teak. In a burst of impatience Feodor blurted, "Good afternoon, Mister Ling, I am here to get my passport. Is it ready?"

Looking up, Ling took the mettle of this impudent fellow with his cheeks swollen and one eye closed. "What passport? I am an honest drafts-man. I do not deal in unlawful enterprises." Ling was older than sixty years. His hair was long and grey, and his eyes jet black. He was dressed in a black gown and wore the traditional skullcap with a red tassel.

Feodor recovered his bearings, squared his shoulders, and said, "My apologies, Mister Ling. My mind is troubled by untoward events. I meant no dishonor." He gently rubbed his face and introduced himself. "I am Feodor Alexandrovich, the person Mister Wuhan spoke to you about late yesterday afternoon."

Ling rose and approached Feodor. "I know Mister Wuhan and his niece, Yen Hei-lan. Why do you bother me about a counterfeit passport? Go away."

With near desperation, Feodor appealed, "Mister Ling, Miss Yen took my photograph in Wuhan's shop yesterday, and his shop girl brought it to you about sundown."

Ling moved closer to Feodor and stared at his face for several seconds. "You've had the pleasure of Yen Hei-lan's company, I notice." He shuffled papers on his desk and withdrew Feodor's photograph. "You are more comely in your photograph. Please tell me in what country is such a passport to be issued?"

"Poland. It is supposed to be a Polish passport in the name of Zinovy Annikov. And Wuhan was to pay for your services."

"Polish, you say. What do I know about Polish passports?"

Impatiently, Feodor said, "Yes, Polish. And in the name Zinovy Annikov."

Ling continued his stare. "Perhaps." A few seconds later, he went to the desk, opened the middle drawer, and withdrew an envelope. He handed it to Feodor. "Your passport is paid for." With a stern voice he demanded, "Leave. I am busy."

Exiting the forger's shop, Feodor ripped open the envelope and examined his exquisitely detailed Polish passport.

Feodor entered the China National Bank and Trust Company and quickly spotted the senior teller's desk. The nameplate read "Mister Chan Sen-tao." He approached and extended his hand to the fellow at the desk. "Good afternoon, Mister Chan. I am Zinovy Annikov. The person Mister Wuhan discussed with you on the telephone yesterday afternoon."

Ignoring Feodor's outstretched hand, Chan carefully appraised his visitor. "Please sit down, Mister Annikov. I have been expecting you." As Feodor settled in, Chan asked, "May I see Mister Wuhan's check and your passport?" Feodor handed these items to him. Chan inspected these documents and saw that they were correct. Unseen by Feodor, Chan pressed a button hidden under his desk. "These seem to be in order. I will give them to the security guard behind you for safekeeping."

Confused and now suspicious, Feodor turned around and saw a uniformed guard standing a few feet from him. His hand was on the pistol in his holster. Feodor faced Chan. "What safekeeping? I want to cash the check as has been arranged and leave this place." In a firm voice, he continued, "Hand me the funds and return my passport."

"Unfortunately, Mister Annikov, or whatever your name is, I cannot do so. Miss Yen Hei-lan, Wuhan's niece and cosigner on this account, has issued a stop-payment order on this check. She told me you obtained it by fraud and coerced her to arrange for the passport under threat of death."

Feodor sputtered in disbelief, "That is utter nonsense. We made an honest deal. I sold Wuhan a valuable necklace at a fair price."

Chan rose and spoke in a firm voice. "I have dealt with the Wuhan family as honorable clients for many years. And I will continue to do so. Your business here is concluded. My security guard will escort you to the door. If it were not for the possibility of a scandal involving this bank and Mister Wuhan, I would have you arrested by the International Police."

Beaten by the perfidy of Black Orchid, Feodor understood that his position was untenable. The thought flashed through his mind that he should have killed her. Unfortunately, it was too late. That vixen's unexpected guile had vanquished him. Moreover, to cause trouble here would destroy anything left of his mission. He had lost the necklace, the passport, and the check. With chaotic thoughts swirling in his head, he meekly let the guard escort him out of the bank.

Dejected and ashamed, Feodor wandered into Tiananmen Square. He found an unoccupied bench and sat. In deep distress, he contemplated his options. None, he understood. He had no necklace, no check, no identification, no funds, and no honor. In addition, in all probability, Black Orchid had vowed to kill him and sent out her goons to find him. He reasoned that he could not return to his hotel or to the restaurant where he normally took his meals. Black Orchid knew the haunts of the White Russian community and most probably had these places watched. Her agents, no doubt, were watching the railroad station.

After an hour, darkness engulfed Peking. Feodor stopped at a noodle shop for a light supper and a cup of green tea. The bill was only two dollars but it reduced the meager amount of his remaining Chinese dollars. Refreshed, his mind's turmoil abated. Suddenly, out of the gloom, his mind cleared to some extent, and he recalled that in the past year, he had pawned his late wife's ivory brooch at a pawnshop in an area just beyond the vicinity of Wuhan's Antiks. It was a magnificent piece with a profile of Empress Alexandra.

Within a few minutes, Feodor approached Tsingtao Street. Not knowing the status of Black Orchid or where she might be, he slunk through the deep shadows of the shops opposite the lane with the Antiks shop. Clear of the danger area, he walked with purpose to the pawnshop, identified only by the universal symbol—three spheres suspended from a bar over the door. Though it had been many months since he had made the deal for the brooch, he wondered if the proprietor, Mister Lio Chung-k'ai, would be there and would remember him.

Feodor entered and the bell on the door tinkled, alerting the man who was inside a steel cage working on his accounts. He looked up and spotted Feodor. A faint memory of a Russian Occidental flashed through his mind, but he could not place the fellow. In deference to his Western clients, Lio was dressed in a smart dark-grey suit. His shop was small, well lighted, and neatly kept. Hanging from the walls was a hodgepodge of unredeemed merchandise for sale: musical instruments, tools of all manner, furs, telescopes. Smaller valuable items were enclosed in a glass-topped case: Leica cameras, collectable postage stamps, gold coins, and medium-priced jewelry. Lio stored his expensive items in a large Diebold safe with a tumbler lock.

Feodor's spirits rose when he recognized the man. "Good evening, Mister Lio. I am pleased to see you again."

Mister Lio rose, went to the opening in the cage, and stared at Feodor for a few seconds. Lio was a short, plump man with grey-speckled hair, square chin, and soft grey eyes. His courtesy barred him from noticing or asking about Feodor's distorted face.

"We have done business before, Occidental?"

"Yes, of course. Last summer, I sold you a magnificent brooch. Do you recall?"

"My mind is old. Events a month or two ago are not clear. Yet your face seems faintly familiar. Tell me your name and more about the brooch."

Feodor understood with absolute clarity that he had to be completely forthright with Lio if he were to succeed.

With intensity, Feodor related, "My name is Feodor Alexandrovich Romanov—nephew to Czar Nicholas II. The brooch belonged to my deceased wife. A Faberge piece. It was about five centimeters tall and featured an exquisitely detailed profile of the Empress Alexandra etched deep into the ivory."

A small smile spread across Lio's face. "Indeed, sir. I remember this splendid brooch—a true work of art by a master craftsman. I am pleased to have been of some assistance." He opened his sales record book and scanned his sales for the summer months of 1935. "Here it is. Now, I recall the sale clearly. A few days after my purchase from you, I sold it to a mandarin from Shansi Province—a large man, with a long white beard, and a beautiful young concubine on his sleeve—a gift for the woman, no doubt." He closed the sales book and understood that Feodor was seriously distressed. He opened the cage door. "Please come in. Let us have tea and be comfortable."

"Thank you, Mister Lio. I am weary in body and mind."

Lio looked at him intensely and wondered what had happened to this fellow.

Feodor entered the main body of the shop and Lio directed him to a small table. Lio poured steaming tea into porcelain cups exquisitely decorated with scenes of the Forbidden City.

"Thank you, Mister Lio, for your hospitality."

"It is my pleasure to ease your obvious discomfort." He looked carefully at Feodor's damaged face. "Please forgive me for being impertinent." He paused for a second or so. "May I inquire how you managed to have your face and eye so damaged?"

Feodor sipped the tea, and after a short pause, asked, "May I be frank with you, Mister Lio?"

"Of course."

"Also, I must have your word that you will keep my visit confidential?"

"Such serious business you must have. Of course. I am the keeper of many secrets."

Feodor continued. "I am in serious trouble and have no one to trust or to ask for help."

"Police trouble?"

"No. Not the police. It is Yen Hei-lan, Black Orchid, your neighbor." With frightful passion in his voice, he added, "She wants to murder me!"

Lio stroked his beard as thoughts whirled in his mind. "Murder? You? I know this woman and her reputation. It is my mind to avoid her. Indeed, you are in serious danger for raising her ire. Why does she want to murder you?"

With a catch in his throat, Feodor continued, "This morning she was convinced that I had a secret about missing Romanov jewels. Despite my protestations that I had no knowledge of them, she tortured me with a syringe full of belladonna to reveal what I could not reveal. Eventually, I was able to strike her forcefully and escape." Some of the pain returned as he recalled his ordeal. He emptied his teacup. "With skillful chicanery, she has cheated me out of a valuable necklace, my newly forged passport, and all my funds. And, I am sure that her ruffians are searching for me. You were the only person I could think of for help."

Lio looked at Feodor for several seconds, evaluating his story. Shortly, he rose, locked the door, and pulled down the door shade. He returned and poured more tea. He took a sip. With his head tilted slightly to one side and a thin smile of understanding, he responded, "I am not surprised. Mistress Yen is a most dangerous person. She is without scruples—a classic sociopath—one never to cross. Her vengeance is merciless. She was responsible for the death of my brother's number-one son two years ago. I avoid doing business with her and her uncle as much as possible." He paused for more tea. "And how may I be of help to my Russian client?" His eyes sparkled with impish mischief.

Sensing hope, Feodor related, "I must leave China. However, without a passport and funds, I am trapped. Nonetheless, with your assistance, I may have an option to recover and escape to a Western country." Slowly and reluctantly, he withdrew the Saint Andrew's medal and the gold chain. Thoughts flashed through his mind of Magdalena and the tender moment when they parted. Carefully, he offered the medal and chain to Lio. "My last fiscal resource is this gold medal keepsake, given to me by a dear friend now gone to Canada."

Lio cocked his head, picked up the gold medal with a jeweler's tweezers, and inspected it with his ten-power loupe. After a minute or so, he said, "I am impressed, my Russian friend." He placed the medal on the table. "Have you noticed the engraving on the back—well worn now, after all these years?"

"I've been wearing it since my friend gave it to me, and I have not thought to inspect it carefully." Feodor picked it up and tried to discern the engraving, without success. He returned it to Lio. "What do you see, Mister Lio?"

"The engraving is faint but readable under my loupe. There is the Russian double-eagle crest. The date is '28 June 1744' and I see the initials 'YA/PHG.'" He put down the medal and the loupe. "My Russian history is weak. What do you make of it?"

Feodor scribbled the initials on a small pad on the table. He reflected for several minutes. "I have it." He smiled broadly at what he had deduced. "This must be a wedding present from Czar Peter III to his bride, Catherine von Anhall-Zerbst Domburg."

Lio, with a quizzical look, asked, "Explain, please."

"The date is their wedding day. 'YA' must stand for Yekaterina Alekseyevna. Catherine had converted to the Orthodox Church and this was her new Russian name. And 'PHG' stands for 'Peter von Holstein-Gottorp.'"

"You're confident that your analysis is correct?"

"Almost one hundred percent."

Lio leaned back in his chair, poured more tea, and took a couple of sips as he evaluated this astounding information. "Indeed, this medal is a rare treasure, and will entice the collectors of Russian antiques."

With sorrow in his voice, Feodor said, "I'm reluctant to sell this medal but I have no choice." He sipped his tea. "Mister Lio, please make an offer."

"Please understand that I am not a buyer of antiques or anything else. As a pawnbroker, I lend money and the borrower deposits with me an item of significantly more value for security. If, within ninety days the borrower does not repay my loan, the property is forfeited to me as compensation for the monetary loss I have incurred."

"Yes, I understand." Feodor leaned toward Lio and continued in an intense voice. "I do not want to pawn this medal. I want to sell it. I must confess, Mister Lio, that I do not have the background to evaluate the value of my medal. My trust is in you. Please make an offer in British pounds sterling."

"A moment, Russian." Lio rose and went to a shelf filled with books. He selected one, flipped the pages, and studied the entries. With a decisive stride, he returned to the table, sat, and filled Feodor's cup. "Frankly, Mister Romanov, I have incomplete knowledge of this medal's value, and I have limited knowledge of the market in such items. Nevertheless, my offer is 500 pounds sterling."

Feodor was disappointed by Lio's offer. "After our discovery of this medal's history and the point that collectors might bid handsomely for it, I would have expected that your offer would be more advanced."

"My Russian friend, if I understood better the market for such items I might make a more handsome offer. Accordingly, my offer stands at 500 pounds sterling. Do you accept?"

Confounded by his desperate situation and with no other options, Feodor said, "Reluctantly, I accept."

Lio picked up the medal and chain and placed them in a chamois bag. He put the bag into his pocket.

"You have made a wise choice." He rose. "I will get your money." Lio opened the safe in the corner, withdrew an envelope, counted out five one-hundred-pound notes, and handed them to Feodor. Both rose and shook hands. Lio asked, "What now, my Russian friend?"

"Mister Lio, I cannot return to my hotel or any other place I've been. By now, I imagine that dozens of Black Orchid's thugs are scouring the city for me." Feodor dropped his eyes, all his bravado dissipated. "I must ask you for more assistance. Will you allow me to sleep in your basement for a few days until I have all the details of my plan in place?"

After reflection, Lio said, "Very well, Occidental. I will bring a cot and a blanket for you."

"Thank you, Mister Lio. I am in your debt. May I impose on your kindness for more help, please?"

Lio stood and said impatiently, "I manage a pawn shop, not a help organization." He walked about for a time. "Do you want that she-devil or her ruffians to kill me? If she discovers I have helped you, my death warrant is signed." He continued pacing about. He returned to the table. "You press my 'treasured client' greeting too far." He poured more tea and took several sips. "I am not of a sound mind. Whatever I am to do for you, my fee is 50 pounds." He pounded the table with his fist, knocking over the teacups. "I take this responsibility only because I dislike and distrust Wuhan and especially his heinous niece. Peking would be a far more hospitable city without them."

Feodor smiled. He had completed a key step for his journey to the West. "Thank you, Mister Lio. I agree."

Feodor and Lio talked far into the night.

Early the next morning, Lio opened the door of the draftsman's shop. He entered and spotted Mister Ling at his drafting table. "Greetings, my fine neighbor Mister Ling. I am delighted to see you in good health this morning. Busy as usual, I see. Excellent for continued profit."

Ling looked up and saw his old friend. "Good morning to you, Mister Lio. Welcome to my shop." He put down his drawing instruments. "It is fortunate that you visit now. I need to have a break from this drawing tedium. Join me with morning tea. Your business is profitable?"

"Indeed. Frequently, it is the White Russians that divest their treasures with me—never to be redeemed. Westerners come to my shop for bargains at vastly inflated prices. Yes. Business is most profitable." For a long time the two friends sipped tea and exchanged gossip from the alley.

Finally, Lio said in an earnest voice, "My dear longtime friend, may I speak to you in confidence and ask for a favor?"

"Of course, my honorable friend. You have my trust. What troubles you?"

"I have a client, a White Russian, who is in serious trouble and is in need of your expertise. At the moment, I have him hidden in my basement."

Ling smiled faintly. "Your countenance this morning is revealing. It is clear that you have serious concerns. What is this trouble of which you speak?"

"The Russian is under the threat of death by Yen Hei-lan."

Ling frowned and shifted in his chair at Yen's name.

"A Lorelei is that beautiful niece of Wuhan. I cringe when she enters my shop to do business. Her presence strikes fear in me. I am afraid that one day she will be the death of me." He rose and went to his drafting table, picked up a triangle, and tapped it slowly on the table. His thoughts swirled.

Lio remained seated and said nothing as his friend considered if he would help the Russian.

Ling returned to the table. "What is in my power to thwart Miss Yen? If I am to help, my participation must be secret. I wish not to wake up with my departed ancestors."

"The Russian needs a passport and a marriage license from the Orthodox Church on Chung Hwa Road here in Peking."

"A passport is but minor trouble. But a marriage license? Tell me more."

"The Russian needs a Polish passport in the name of Zinovy Annikov."

"Your request confuses me. Yesterday Alexandrovich Romanov was here to get such a passport in that name, Zinovy Annikov. Why another one?"

"His passport was stolen from him by an associate of Mistress Yen."

Ling's eyes narrowed and he frowned deeply as a ripple of fear cascaded down his spine. "I see." He tapped a triangle on his desk for several seconds. "And in what names is the marriage license?"

"Zinovy Annikov and Magdalena Ivanovna Makarenko." Lio wrote the names on a scrap of paper. "The date should be 25 July 1917. The Russian needs an original and a duplicate."

"This may pose some difficulties." He turned away from Lio and looked out the window at the bustle in the alley. Finally, he concluded that he would do almost anything to thwart that she-devil. "I will send my number-two son to the church's rectory to offer some compensation to the manager for blank forms and a document with the priest's signature. If all goes well, I will have these documents ready in a few days. My fee for helping the Russian is 25 pounds."

"Your fee is reasonable. I will return this afternoon with payment."

Late that afternoon, Feodor sat at a small table in Lio's basement and drafted a cablegram. His spirits were elated that the second phase of his plan was underway. He wrote:

To Magdalena Ivanovna Makarenko, 14 A Prince Royal Street, Vancouver, Canada.

MAGDALENA UNTOWARD EVENTS FORCE ME TO LEAVE CHINA STOP I NEED YOUR HELP STOP I DO NOT WANT TO DISTURB THE LIFE YOU HAVE MADE FOR YOURSELF IN CANADA STOP YOU ARE THE ONLY PERSON I KNOW IN THE WEST STOP IF YOU AGREE I WILL MAIL A MARRIAGE LICENSE IN YOUR NAME AND MY NEW NAME ZINOVY ANNIKOV STOP USE THIS LICENSE TO ARRANGE FOR MY IMMIGRATION PAPERS TO CANADA AS YOUR HUSBAND STOP EXPLAIN THE FIFTEEN-YEAR GAP SAY WE WERE SEPARATED IN THE CHAOS OF THE REVOLUTION AND ONLY RECENTLY MADE CONTACT THROUGH MUTUAL FRIENDS STOP IF YOU AGREE CONTACT ME AT GENERAL DELIVERY AMERICAN EXPRESS SHANGHAI STOP FEODOR

Should Magdalena agree with his plan, he had decided, he would send her the marriage license and copies of his Polish passport and supporting documents via airmail on Pan American World Airways' China Clipper. He understood that it would take a couple of months or more for her to arrange for his immigration papers. He realized that he did not have sufficient finances for his living expenses during the long wait in Shanghai and for the purchase of his steamship ticket to Vancouver. He speculated, "Perhaps I could find a job as a gardener with one of the business families in the International Settlement."

Three days later, Ling delivered the documents in a large envelope. Lio checked them and saw that they were nearly perfect. Lio sent his number-two son to the Radio Corporation of America's cable office with Feodor's cablegram.

Later, Lio entered his basement holding the envelope and addressed Feodor as he handed it to him. "Russian, Mister Ling has delivered your documents."

"Thank you, Mister Lio," said Feodor as he opened the envelope and carefully inspected the documents. "They are excellent."

"All work by Mister Ling is excellent. My sons have visited the train station and they are convinced that Yen's ruffians still are watching it."

Feodor, in a near shout of dismay, lamented, "I am confined in Peking! Is there no way for me to leave?"

"Here is my last action to help you, Russian. Your fee of fifty pounds sterling is exhausted. This evening my number-one son will drive you to the train station at Wanping—some twenty miles south of here. At about 2100, the local night train from Peking to Shanghai will stop there for a few minutes. Then you will be on your own."

"Mister Lio, I am unable to express my appreciation for your hospitality and assistance. Thank you."

Turning to leave the basement, Lio spoke. "I do not know you. I have never seen you."

In the obituary column of the English language newspaper *Peking Daily Chronicle* the following the following week appeared a notice of interest.

"Mister Lio Chung-k'ai, proprietor of a pawnshop on Tsingtao Street, and his two sons yesterday were found dead hanging from rafters in his shop.

Mister Ling Ping-shu, proprietor of a drafting shop on Tsingtao Street, was found dead, sprawled across his drafting table. An autopsy revealed he died of acute poisoning from cobra venom. Chief Inspector Reginald

Fawcett-Smythe of the International Police confirmed that inquiries are continuing."

Afterword

Dear Reader, the mysterious deaths of Lio Chung-kai and Mister Ling Ping-shu were never solved. Two years later, Chief Inspector Reginald Fawcett-Smythe transferred to the constabulary in Singapore and, after a few months, his open-case files were sent to the archives, where they remained untouched.

Last year, whilst on assignment in Beijing, I reviewed the cold-case file on these murders as background for my new film script. To experience the ambiance of the scene, I wandered down one of those narrow alleys that are lined with a myriad of small specialty shops that offer sundry wares, so common in the older sections of Chinese cities. Shortly, I spotted a weather-beaten wood sign with faded lettering, hung at a severely crooked angle. It read "Antiks."

Intrigued, I opened the door to this old and somewhat dilapidated antique shop. An ol' time bell tinkled as I entered the dark and musty shop. Hanging from the low ceiling was an elec¬tric cord with a single, bare light bulb—the sole illumination. The place was jammed with tourist junk—some of which, I suspected, had been in the bins for many years. A grimy movie poster on the wall hawked Howard Hughes' film Hell's Angels, staring Jean Harlow and Ben Lyon.

A stooped, wizened-faced woman shuffled into the room and made a short bow. Seeing that I was an Occidental, she waved her hand slightly, indicating that I could pe¬ruse her stock at will. Squeezing down an aisle, I spotted a large bin jammed with "stuff": old photographs, philatelic material, prints, and paintings. Being a China stamp collector, I selected several Qing Dynasty covers with the red revenue stamps overprinted with large Arabic numerals. Digging deep¬er into this "treasure trove," I pulled out a portrait of a strikingly beautiful young woman in a red cheongsam. I stared at this portrait for a minute or so—mesmerized by her bewitching pose and erotic mien. The menace in her eyes conveyed that she was a gravely dangerous woman.

I wondered if the female in this portrait was the fantasy of the artist or had once lived. A fantasy, no doubt. On impulse, I turned the portrait over and saw a deeply faded caption scribbled in English. I put on my glasses and moved under the light to read the caption. I gasped in disbelief. The woman was Yen Hei-lan!

Quietly, the old woman slipped out of the room.

Gadzooks! The artist had portrayed Yen exactly as I would have envisioned her. What wizardry was this? Now, I wondered again, was Yen a real person or a fantasy? Was this clairvoyance or serendipity or something else? I stared at the portrait. This ravishing enchantress's perfidy leaped from the drawing. Shortly, I reasoned, What the hell. I'll never know the answer. I looked for the proprietress. She had disappeared. I left a five-pound note on the bin. The bell tinkled softly as I exited the shop with the philatelic covers, and Yen Hei-lan safely tucked under my arm.

Should your curiosity be piqued about Yen's adventures, may I suggest you read my historical adventure titled St. Catherine's Crown—available on Amazon Kindle and other venues. Be cautious, however. Keep Yen Hei-lan at arm's length.

FIN

ABOUT THE AUTHOR

Captain Sylvester M. Shelton is retired from active and reserve U.S. Navy service. He served in Korea, French Indochina, Vietnam, and other areas in the Western Pacific. He has an extensive background in Far East studies.

During his career, Shelton published extensively in trade magazines, peer-reviewed journals, and commercial publications. His professional book, *Communicating Ideas with Film, Video, and Multimedia*, garnered the Best of Show award in the Society for Technical Communication's Spotlight Publication Competition.

Since retirement, he has published several historical, action-adventure novels whose *mise en scène* is the Far East and Africa. The narratives are focused on little known yet critically important events in the early twentieth century, and are consistent with the theatre of the times.

His novellas and short stories comprise a mélange of tales of aviators, assassins, and adventurers. His monographs encompass studies on topics such as photographic optics, Ho Chi Minh and the OSS, and Amelia Earhart.

Details of his literary work are posted on his website:

www.sheltoncomm.com

www.ingramcontent.com/pod-product-compliance
Lightning Source LLC
Chambersburg PA
CBHW041751010726
47507CB00009B/356